love bites

MATED TO THE KING

LOLA GLASS

To my husband
For listening to me ramble on about vampires and sirens and at least *pretending* to think I'm funny

BLAIR

THE ACHE in my head seemed to pound with the beat of the music, like a nail driving deeper into my brain with every moment. Lights pulsed around us, making me wish I could leave the nightclub.

But, I couldn't.

I pushed my way through the crowd, heading toward the bar. Though I was physically ill with hunger, the idea of feeding on a stranger was just as revolting as always. I'd pushed it off as long as I could, but eventually, one of my sisters would bring a guy over and force me to have my way with him.

Not sexually.

As a siren, I had to kiss someone to feed on their emotions. It was usually unpleasant for me, but there was no avoiding it if I wanted to stay alive.

My gaze caught on an empty seat straight in front of me. I headed toward it, ignoring a hand that brushed my shoulder and someone who called behind me, "Hey, blondie!"

They could screw off.

It wasn't my fault I'd been born with golden hair. And while I usually liked that about myself, I was annoyed by the assumptions that came with it.

Then again, my entire family was annoyed by the assumptions that clung to us like last month's gallon of milk, stinking up everything. Being a siren meant being physically appealing to all people, human or magical, and that was nowhere near as fun as it sounded.

The city we lived in, Mistwood, was the capital and only real city in the magical world. We were completely hidden from humans, outside of the goods they shipped to us.

Everyone in the club was magical like us, though sirens were particularly known for having magic that made us vulnerable in too many ways.

At least vampires had teeth.

We were just their weaker, prettier equivalent.

Not that vampires were ugly. They were known for being supernaturally gorgeous, too. Then again, all magical beings were.

I plopped down on my seat, massaging my temples as my body screamed at me for fighting my hunger too long.

"Are you okay?" The man in the seat beside mine lifted his voice over the music. It was so loud, my ears strained to pick out the words.

"Peachy," I called back, not bothering to look over at him. He was undoubtedly already feeling the pull of my bitchy magic.

"What can I get you?" the bartender asked.

A sharp pain in my head made me wince. I couldn't have answered him if I wanted to.

Thankfully, the song that was on ended, and a slightly quieter one began.

"Get her a glass of water with peppermint," the man beside me said.

Though I knew he was only helping me because of my bitchy magic, I appreciated the gesture anyway.

He was right; I did need water. And peppermint leaves. They were one of the only things that could dull a siren's hunger, for absolutely no logical reason. It had something to do with the way our magic worked.

The bartender slid the glass to me a moment later, and I grabbed it with one hand, still pressing hard against my temple with my other thumb.

I took a slow, long drink, and my headache subsided just the tiniest bit.

I'd been drowning myself in peppermint for nearly two

weeks, so the effect was nowhere near what it should've been. That was my fault, though.

"Thanks," I said, finally looking at the guy who'd helped me.

I sucked in a breath at the sight of him.

Magical beings, in general, were more attractive than humans. We were stronger, our men were taller, and our power kept us physically healthy and toned no matter what we ate or if we exercised.

But this guy was something else altogether.

His eyes were a piercing shade of blue that somehow put me at ease, and his face was perfectly balanced. Not too sharp, and not too soft. He had light skin and dark hair cut precisely, and he'd styled it like it was art. The blue button-down shirt he had on was undone at the top, open just enough to be appealing without screaming, *DOUCHEBAG*.

Something about him looked kind of familiar, but I couldn't figure out why.

"No problem. What's an unmated siren doing at a night-club?" he asked, looking more curious than anything.

I got the same question every time I left my house, so his curiosity didn't surprise me in the slightest. There weren't very many sirens, and most of us were treated more like objects than people much of the time. Usually, we were mated to powerful people very young to prevent us from being used and abused.

The woman on my other side turned toward me and set her hand on my thigh. I pushed it away, turning closer to the guy. He seemed to be able to fight the pull of my magic, at the very least.

I took another long drink of my water before admitting, "It's been almost a month since I've fed. I had no choice but to come here."

"That's a long time to fight your nature."

"My nature can go fuck itself."

I finished my glass and set it back down on the countertop. The guy next to me waved the bartender down, and I thanked him when he brought me a fresh glass.

The bartender smiled, leaning over the bar toward me.

My magic would be working on him too.

I leaned away, and the guy next to me patted the bartender on the arm. "This one's mine, Thor. Find someone else."

Usually, the words would've set off an alarm in my head, but I could tell the guy was just trying to protect me. And I appreciated that.

The bartender grumbled, but turned around.

"Thanks." I picked up my second glass of water, but didn't drink it right away.

"No problem." My protector studied me. "What's your name?"

"Blair. You?"

"Damian." The name fit. I liked it. "I've got a proposition for you, Blair."

"Wow. And you were doing *so* well."

He chuckled. "Not that kind of proposition. You clearly don't like feeding. Neither do I." He flashed me a peek of his fangs, revealing himself as a vampire. "I can drink from blood bags to avoid it, but you can't. If you need a food source tonight, I can be that. No strings attached, and no expectations to follow. My magic will make it less unpleasant for you."

I studied him suspiciously, waiting for the other shoe to drop.

He was right—vampire magic put their prey at ease while a siren's riled up their food source. Even if he didn't drink from me, I could benefit from his power and erase my hunger too.

"What's in it for you?" I finally asked.

He lifted a shoulder. "I've never felt a siren's magic before."

I probably should've said no... but it seemed like a better option than waiting for one of my sisters to drag someone over to feed me.

So, I sighed. "Alright, deal."

I set my glass back down and slipped off my stool, throwing a leg over his lap and taking a seat there. Kissing tall guys while standing was uncomfortable, considering I was barely 5'1".

His erection didn't surprise me in the slightest. My magic had that effect on people. At least Damian didn't seem like he expected anything from me because of it.

"I have a room here, if it would make you more comfortable," he said, sliding a hand slowly up my lower back. The touch sent his magic moving through me, relaxing my body immediately.

Any vampire could get a room in any of Mistwood's nightclubs if they filled out the paperwork. The nightclubs were made for them, after all. Owned by them, too. Their leader —he was a king, even if he refused to let anyone call him that—was well known for checking in on his clubs and vampires. I'd never met him, but he was supposed to be terrifying.

"It's fine. Everyone around us already knows what I am anyway," I said.

His magic continued easing the nerves in my abdomen. And as they eased, my hunger flared.

I grabbed his shirt by the collar. The fabric felt nice in my hands, but I chalked that up to his power too. "A girl could get addicted to the feel of your magic."

"The right girl, maybe."

His words didn't set in, because as soon as he was done speaking, my mouth was on his.

His lips parted for me without hesitation. Our tongues brushed lightly, and I groaned at the taste of him. Not the taste of his mouth—though that was nice—but the taste of his emotions.

Amusement.

Excitement.

Desire.

My magic spurred them higher, devouring the surface-level feelings and digging in deeper until I found what I really craved.

Exhaustion.

Boredom.

Loneliness.

Pain.

Overwhelm.

I could feel one of his hands pressing into my lower back as we made out, pulling me against him harder. The other had made its way to my hair, and felt good gripping the strands tightly.

There was a sudden prick of pain on my lip, and I moaned when his emotions shifted abruptly.

Lust.

Need.

Pleasure.

Hope.

Someone shook my shoulder, but I barely felt it.

"The wolves are here, Blair," a familiar female voice urged, and my shoulder shook again. "The Alpha showed up for Clem. We have to go, now."

The wolves.

The Alpha.

Clem...

I ripped my mouth away from Damian's.

His blue eyes blazed with bloodlust, and I ran my tongue over the cut on my lip. "You bit me."

"You—" he began, but I turned to my sister. Avery was beside me, her expression dark and worried. She was one of my four sisters, and though we weren't related by blood, we were family through and through.

"I have to go. Thanks for this." I gestured between me and Damian as I tried to slide off his lap.

His hand pressed harder against my lower back, holding me in place even though he released my hair. "I can't—"

Avery grabbed my glass of peppermint water off the countertop and splashed it at him.

I took his moment of surprise to push his hand away from me, and she helped tug me off his lap.

Adrenaline pumped through me as we threw ourselves into the crowd, letting the heights of the magical men conceal us from my blue-eyed meal. We were just as fast as vampires when we'd been fed, so he wouldn't catch us if we didn't let him.

But no one could run through a crowd of magical beings. Too many of them would be triggered by the urge to chase.

The satisfaction of not being hungry anymore was enough to put a smile on my face. And for once, I didn't regret feeding on someone.

Damian was... well, delicious.

"Everyone else is in the car already," Avery called to me, as we finally emerged from the crowd.

"How bad was it?"

She grimaced. The flashing lights above us highlighted her olive skin and long, dark brown hair, but all I really noticed was the worry in her eyes. "Bad."

I didn't ask anything else.

I'd find out soon enough.

And though I was worried about my sister, Damian's magic somehow seemed to be lingering in my system. I felt like everything was going to be okay, even though logically I knew that probably wasn't the case.

That didn't make sense, so I chalked it up to not feeling hungry for the first time in a month, and moved on.

We had bigger problems than the vampire who had fed me.

two

BLAIR

THE OTHER GIRLS had our minivan waiting on the curb just outside the club. We got in quickly, and Izzy peeled away from the building.

"What happened?" I asked, turning on the seat to look at my sisters in the back. Clementine's eyes were watering, her pale skin flushed, and her red hair flattened around her face. Zora was hugging her fiercely, though her tan skin was almost as pale as Clem's. Her curly, cinnamon-colored hair was up in a bun.

And despite my question, I knew the answer as soon as I saw them.

Because on the center of Clementine's neck, there was a big, bold mating mark.

Starting a mate bond was easy.

Really easy.

All it took was a brush of your hand to someone's neck, a little spike of magic, and a three-word declaration.

You are mine.

Unless the magic user envisioned a prettier marking, the default one that appeared was a thick, navy-blue stripe that circled your neck like a magical choker. It felt like a new tattoo, barely raised from the skin, but there was no way to remove it.

If the bond wasn't reciprocated, it would disappear—after an entire year. If it was, the blue turned black and became permanent.

Mating was our society's version of marriage, but the magical connection was much more than a vow and a signature.

Clementine's wasn't one of the pretty, elegant markings I'd seen on the few mated beings I'd met. It was the ugly, basic mark of a man who didn't give a damn about his "mate's" throat or confidence.

A basic mate mark was little more than a brand.

And this brand was from a cruel, dangerous bastard who had been chasing my sister for far too long.

"He grabbed her from behind," Zora said, as Clem's tears started falling harder. She was shaking—and I didn't blame her. I would've been shaking too. "We pulled her away, but he'd already started the bond. The mark appeared on our way to the van."

"He's still in there?" I demanded. "I will fucking *kill* him."

"He has too many of his wolves with him. We only got away because he let us," Izzy said from the driver's seat. "If you go back in there, you'll get mated to another one of them."

"I should've been with you," I said, my fists clenching.

Of the five of us, I was the only one who had been taught how to fight. I'd been trying to teach them for years, but my lessons had happened when I was so young that they were instincts more than anything else. I was a useless teacher.

And signing up for public classes was like telling all of the magical beings in the world where to find us, which was just flat-out stupid.

Sirens were weak, but we were valuable. When we fed on people, it made them feel alive. Helped them cope with their emotions, too. For immortal beings, that was a priceless gift.

One that many of the strongest and worst wanted to claim for themselves.

Hence the arranged matings that were common for our kind.

But our mothers had all been trapped in unhappy mate bonds. They protected us from the same fate, even though it put them in danger and eventually led to their deaths.

My sisters and I had managed to get to the safehouse they'd prepared after they were killed, and we'd basically been in hiding ever since. We'd made it ten years, starting businesses from our home and only leaving when we had no other choice.

But we had to go out to eat.

And that was when the wolves had found us.

There were hundreds, if not thousands, of werewolf packs scattered throughout the world, but most of them were fairly small. The main wolf pack was in Mistwood.

And it was bigger than any of the others, by a long, long way.

Because Mistwood was the capital of the magical world, the five most powerful beings (one of every type) were located there. They were basically the kings of our world, though they rejected the term *kings* and insisted they were called *leaders*.

All five of them were men, by some obnoxious twist of fate.

Their images circled frequently, and I'd heard that people fell all over them everywhere they went. I'd never paid much attention to the pictures I'd seen of them. Everyone knew their names, though.

Talon was the dragon king.

Curtis was the werewolf king.

Hale was the vampire king.

Kai was the fae king.

And Bane was the monster king.

Curtis was the only one we'd actually met, and people defi-nitely fell all over him. We met him for the first time a few months earlier, at a different nightclub, and had been avoiding him ever since. He'd tried to convince us to join his pack at first, then tried to offer us money in exchange for it. When that didn't work, he'd proposed mating, for the sake of our "protection".

Clementine was the best of us, socially. She'd been taught to use her magic to make a conversation go her way. Izzy had too, she just refused to do it.

After we watched Curtis kill a bartender just for making his drink wrong, Clementine had used a *lot* of it.

Anyway, Clem was the one he'd wanted from the beginning. As much as it frustrated us, there was nothing we could do to change that or stop it. And after we turned him down, he went on the attack.

We'd been hiding from him ever since, but we still had to feed. And apparently, he'd caught us.

"No, you needed to eat," Clem said quietly, wiping her eyes. "It's fine. We'll be okay. Right?"

"Of course we will," Avery said, nodding. "We're going to figure it out."

She looked at me.

Izzy glanced at me in the rearview mirror, turning down a street that didn't lead to our house.

Because of the bond, Curtis would be able to track Clem's physical location, so we couldn't go home.

Clem looked at me, and Zora did too.

Their gazes and our past experiences told me that they expected *me* to figure it out. My mom had been the leader of our mothers' group, so I supposed it was natural that the role fell to me, even if I didn't want it any more than my sisters did.

I let out a slow breath.

We couldn't go home, and we had nowhere else to go.

Hotels weren't safe for sirens. People could feel our magic through the walls. And even if that was an option, Curtis could've tracked Clem there.

Which left us with exactly one option:

I said, "We have to go to the Manor."

The Manor wasn't actually a manor.

It wasn't even a castle.

It was *five* monstrous buildings, large enough to house hundreds to thousands of magical beings each, with another massive structure in the middle that connected all of them and housed even more people. There was one building for each type of magical being, ruled by its leader.

Whoever named it the *Manor* was a moron. Or just didn't know what to call it any more than I did.

It was basically a city of its own, positioned right at the center of Mistwood.

"There's no other option," Avery agreed, her jaw set in a grimace.

"I could go to Curtis. You guys could go home," Clem whispered. "It's your best chance of survival. If we go to the Manor, they could hand all of us to him."

"We're not doing that," Zora said flatly.

"Definitely not," I agreed. "We're technically ruled by the vampires, since they're the strongest beings with parasitic magic. Hale will get to decide what happens to us, regardless of Clem's mate bond. We don't know him—he could be better than Curtis."

Or he could be worse.

We had no idea.

Izzy raked a hand through her long, wavy platinum hair. Her skin was light brown, and her eyes were a deep, soulful shade of green. "It's a risk."

"Better a risk than a death sentence," I said.

"Truer words have never been spoken," Avery murmured.

"Is everyone in agreement?" I looked around the van. It wasn't the fanciest of vehicles, but it got the job done and prevented anyone from looking twice at us.

"Yes," Zora said firmly.

Avery nodded.

"I still think you guys should leave me and go home," Clementine whispered.

"She doesn't count right now," Izzy said quickly. "And I'm in too."

She turned down a street, and the Manor's impressiveness towered in front of us.

"You've been headed there the whole time?" Zora asked, with a snort.

"How many times have I told you to just take charge yourself if you already have a plan?" I grumbled at her.

Izzy winked at me through the mirror. "You're better at it."

I flipped her off, and earned a choked laugh from Clementine. That alone made it worth it.

"We should probably hurry, in case he's already coming after us," Zora said, as Izzy parked in the lot next to the beginning of the dramatic walking path that led to the Manor's center. No one could drive there; the kings wanted everyone to take in the expanse of their power as they walked over a mile to their doorstep.

"We don't need to," Avery said, her eyes fixed on the buildings ahead of us. "I know his type. He thinks he's won. He wants us scared and running from him, and won't feel like he needs to show his face until we've had time to fear him."

Avery was the only one of us who had ever been in a serious relationship before. She didn't talk about it much, but we all knew the basics.

She had thought he loved her, but he'd been using her from the beginning.

Thankfully, she'd escaped before he marked her. Otherwise, we would've been in a similar situation in the past.

"I agree. If he came right after us, it would look desperate, and he doesn't want his pack to see him that way," Clementine said quietly. Her fingers brushed the mark on her neck, and pain flickered in her eyes.

Zora quickly grabbed one of her arms, and Avery grabbed the other, telling her she wasn't alone.

"We should still move as fast as we can without triggering anyone's chase instincts," Izzy said, her gaze flicking around us. There were a few groups of people in the parking lot, and I could see more on the wide path ahead of us. "If any of these people realize what we are, we could be royally screwed."

The rest of us agreed, and headed off.

I was at the front of the group, with Izzy at the back. She watched for anyone coming from behind, and I kept an eye on the front. When she worried about a certain group, she just called my name, and I joined her in the back for a few minutes.

No one made a move against us, thankfully.

IT TOOK NEARLY HALF an hour to reach the center building at our annoyingly slow human pace. Moving supernaturally fast was a siren gift that we all appreciated —but one that didn't do us any good when we couldn't risk anyone chasing us.

I let out a breath of relief when we made it up the stairs and through the massive double doors that opened into the building at the center of the Manor. It was neutral territory, and therefore, should've been safe.

Nothing was a guarantee in our world, but that was about as close as we could get to one.

Inside, the building looked like a castle. The walls were a pristine shade of cream, the light brown stone flooring glittering. The art throughout the room looked expensive, and there were large statues and plants placed strategically to create flow in what was basically a wide-open space with thirty-foot ceilings.

Directly in front of us, there was an oversized receptionist desk that could've held twenty people comfortably. I only saw three openings in it, so it seemed safe to say it was only actually made for three receptionists.

The man sitting in front of one of them was the only person there at the moment.

Forcing myself to walk with confidence I really didn't possess in the situation, I strode across the room. My sisters followed.

"What can I do for you?" the man asked, looking bored.

Another group came in behind us, laughing about something as they headed to the right, toward what I'd thought looked like an elevator on the way in.

"My sister was forcefully bonded to a werewolf, and now our safety is at risk. We're looking for protection," I said, hoping that was something along the lines of what he needed to hear.

"File a claim with the mate committee when they open in the morning." He gestured toward a window, still uninterested in the conversation.

"We can't. We're unmated sirens," I said.

Suddenly, I had his full attention.

"I'll need to see the marking."

Clementine stepped up to him, and he pulled out a flashlight, running it over her throat. The blue of the dark line stood out more beneath the light, proving it wasn't yet permanent.

"This happened in Mistwood?" he asked.

"Yes," she whispered. "At the Red Ring nightclub."

He turned off his flashlight. "I'll need to get in touch with one of the vampires in Hale's inner circle. They're the only ones who can decide whether or not to intervene. You can leave me with your number, or wait there." He gestured to a large section of chairs, lined up carefully.

"We'll wait," I said. "How long will it take?"

He shrugged. "The vampires usually answer immediately, unlike some of the other types, but the decision will likely be Hale's. The vampires have an important competition going on right now, as well as some large-scale renovations, so it could be a few weeks until he sees your request."

"We don't have time," I said. "Is there anything we can do to speed it up?"

"No. I'll try to convey the necessity of moving quickly, but I can't guarantee anything."

"Thank you," I said, and we made our way to the chairs together.

None of us said a word as we waited.

We watched the receptionist—Johnny—make one call. And another. And another.

An hour had passed when a tall, elegant woman with a mate mark around her throat joined Johnny at his desk. He waved us over, and we all went back.

"I'll need you to prove your magic," the woman said to Clementine, not politely but not cruelly either. She ignored the rest of us.

Clem nodded, and I felt the light brush of her power as she put it into the air.

The woman sucked in a breath. "Definitely a siren. Alright." She looked at all of us. "It'll be a few weeks before I can get your case to Hale. Sirens usually live in pods, so is it correct to assume the five of you want to stay together?"

We all nodded.

"I'll make sure to note that on the request. I understand the danger that a forced mate bond can pose to all of you," she said, then looked at Clementine. "I can give you a room in our wing of the Manor until Hale reviews the situation. Your sisters won't be allowed in until he makes a judgment, unfortunately. I assume they have a safe place to stay until then?"

She looked at me.

I nodded, though my stomach clenched at the idea of leaving Clem behind.

"The wolves after us are watching the nightclubs," Izzy said. "We won't be able to risk feeding there without protection."

Which meant starving.

I was used to that, but my sisters weren't. They usually fed every week, like sirens were supposed to.

"I understand, but this is the best I can do until Hale gets a chance to look at everything. You should survive a month and a half without food, right?"

Survive was a loose term, but we could technically do it.

"Yes," I admitted.

"I will make absolutely sure that it's handled before then," she promised. "Now, if you'll come with me..." she gestured to Clementine, who nodded.

She gave us all quick hugs, then followed the vampire woman toward a set of large doors off to the side of the room.

We all watched them go.

Johnny gave us a case number and his contact information, promising to update us weekly on whether he'd heard anything.

With an entirely new reason to worry, the four of us headed back through the doors and made the long walk back to our van.

Clementine texted us pictures of her new room before we got back, which lifted our spirits a little.

But it would be a long few weeks.

three

DAMIAN

I DRUMMED my fingers on my desk, my blood still pumping and my nose still bleeding from my last fight.

Every year, I held a month-long tournament to determine which of my vampires had grown strong enough to join the protective team I ran. And every year, I fought each of the finalists.

I won every fight, of course.

But this time, I'd been distracted.

My thoughts were full of a golden-haired siren.

I still won the fights, but my heart wasn't in them, and everyone could tell.

I'd started searching for Blair the moment she disappeared in that club. My teams combed the city around it, but the woman had vanished.

My taste for blood went with her.

Any blood but hers, that is.

Being a vampire meant bloodlust, constantly. Intense, vicious bloodlust. We kept it sated by feeding regularly, usually from other magical beings who would heal and regenerate much faster than humans. It kept us strong, too.

The only time in my life that my hunger had faded was when I had her taste on my tongue.

I'd had a few blissful, peaceful hours afterward, and I wanted to go back to that so bad it hurt.

Which meant I needed her. Permanently.

I had every vampire I could spare looking for her through the tournament, and none of them had found a thing. She wasn't in the public records. She wasn't online.

The woman was a ghost.

I couldn't tell them that she was a siren, for her safety, so they had to look into every single woman named Blair in Mistwood.

Now that the fights were over, I could finally put the full force of my efforts into finding her.

My office doors opened, and my sister came striding into the room. "It's time to deal with this," she said, patting the top of a massive stack of paperwork.

"Not now." The words came out with a growl.

She tossed me a box of tissues, but I threw it back.

"Your nose is bleeding, Hale."

"How many times do I have to ask you to call me by my first name, Lou?" I grumbled.

"It's too hard to switch back and forth in public and private, and you don't want everyone else calling you Damian, so I refuse for your sake." She set the stack of papers down on my desk. "I know you want to look for your mystery woman, but this can't wait any longer. People's lives are at risk."

"You can handle it."

"Why are you so obsessed with this female?" she asked, leaning closer.

I finally lifted my gaze from my computer screen.

The two of us hadn't had a chance to talk privately since the tournament started, and I'd met Blair a few days after that. Louise had kept everything running for me while I enjoyed the fights.

Or she tried to, at least.

A few of the others I had keeping my wing of the Manor afloat had quit for various reasons during the tournament, which made that an impossible feat.

"Blair is my blood mate. And she's a siren," I said bluntly. "The longer she spends away from me, the more likely I lose her to someone else. Those lives are just going to have to stay at risk, because there's only one I care about right now." I refocused on my computer screen.

A vampire only had one blood mate. He or she was the single person in the world whose blood could dull the constant lust and hunger that otherwise consumed us. We could function despite our bloodlust, but we would never have peace while it raged.

Lou had found hers, Egan, a century earlier. He had become my best friend and the only other member of my inner circle soon enough.

But he had been working with Lou while I dealt with the tournament, so I hadn't told him the truth about Blair yet either.

"Holy shit," Lou said, grabbing her stack of papers again. I expected her to tell me she'd get out of my hair and let me find my female, but the woman didn't budge.

"I'm going to go start knocking on doors if I can't find her soon," I said, glaring at the screen. "She has to be *somewhere*. I had our tech team create an ongoing visual search, so I should know if she takes a step anywhere with a public camera. It shouldn't be this hard to find her. I—"

"*I* found her," Louise hissed. She pulled a folder out of her stack and shoved it at me. "Look."

I opened the folder and scanned the list of contacts, finding a *Blair Davidson* at the top.

"How do you know she's a siren? This could be any of the other Blairs we found," I said. "I—"

"Read the case, asshole."

I read it, swore viciously, and stood up. My heart pounded like a drum in my chest and ears.

My mate was seeking refuge.

She was in hiding.

One of her sisters was already living in my wing of the Manor, hiding from some asshole wolf shifter.

She was in danger, and I hadn't known.

"There's no address listed here. Where do I find her?"

"Sirens don't give out their addresses. You need to have reception call her in, apologize for not reading her case sooner, and do everything you can to make it right," Lou said. "If this woman turns you down, you're screwed. And not in a fun way, Hale."

I gritted my teeth. "She could still turn me down. I'll have to think of a way to ensure she agrees to be mine."

"Talk to Johnny at reception. He saw more of their dynamics than I did, and has been staying in contact with them."

My anger flared at the thought of the receptionist communicating regularly with *my* mate.

I'd get every ounce of information out of him—and then, I'd make Blair mine.

Permanently.

four

BLAIR

I FLOATED on my back in the water, waiting for my phone to ding with a text from Johnny. It took effort, but I was pointedly ignoring the hunger gnawing in my middle and pounding in my head.

My sisters were all at the bottom of our indoor pool. It wasn't huge, but it was about eight feet deep.

The humans' mermaid lore was based on sirens, though we didn't actually have tails. We just needed water. A lot of water. We could breathe it the same way we could breathe air.

We needed peppermint leaves too, though that hadn't made it into the stories.

There was a leaf on my tongue at the moment, actually.

The four of us had been intensely productive the first day after we left Clementine with the vampires. We made our money through a handful of online shops that we ran together, and we needed to get through our assload of orders so we were ready when the vampire king deigned to call us back.

We'd gotten through them within five days.

After that, we made some more things and sold them as-is, to stay busy.

By the time the third week was over, though, my sisters were useless. They weren't used to starving. They were so out of it, they'd barely left the pool at all.

We'd nearly reached week five, and I was drained too. I was used to going a month or so without feeding, but I'd felt like I was in withdrawal since I walked away from Damian. My sisters had teased me about it, but none of them seemed to understand how seriously it was bothering me.

I wasn't just hungry—I was craving *him*.

And the cravings were so intense, I'd started to wonder if they would ever fade at all.

My phone started to ring on the side of the pool, and hope flooded me.

No one at the Manor had ever called before.

Johnny usually just texted.

I answered the call from an unknown number just before it stopped ringing, with a breathless, "Hello?"

"Is this Blair Davidson?" a masculine voice asked. It sounded a little familiar, though I couldn't place it.

"Yes."

"The vampires are ready to see you. A protective team will be waiting for you and your sisters in the Manor's parking lot."

"Thank you." The relief that rolled through me was immense.

My sisters wouldn't last much longer without feeding, and I —well, I didn't really matter. I wasn't sure I'd be able to feed on anyone but Damian again, and I had no way to find him.

Maybe I'd get lucky and he would live at the Manor or something.

"Come quickly, and don't bother packing your things," the man said, before he hung up the phone.

I grabbed one of the painted rocks we used to call each other to the surface, and tossed it into the water. My sisters made their way up, though they didn't move anywhere near fast.

"The vampires are ready," I said, my heart beating fast.

"Thank fuck," Izzy groaned.

"Finally," Zora mumbled.

Avery just crossed the pool and climbed out. Her arms shook a little, so I pulled her up. Despite my intense cravings, I wasn't weak from hunger the way my sisters were. I chalked that up to my past experiences with starving.

None of them had the energy to get dressed, so I just grabbed their swimsuit coverups. I pulled mine over my head, then grabbed the van's keys. My sisters all piled in, sagging against doors and windows, so I took the driver's seat.

"How do you do this all the time?" Izzy asked me, mumbling the words from where her face was pressed to the passenger window.

"I don't like kissing strangers," I said with a shrug.

"Kissing is fun," Zora grumbled.

"There will be plenty of vampires to kiss at the Manor," I said.

It wasn't a guarantee, but I had to be hopeful. Otherwise, the fear might break me.

WE MADE it to the parking lot soon enough, and my eyes widened as I pulled in.

There wasn't a small protective team waiting for us—there were lines of at least three dozen vampires on the sidewalk and in the road.

Before I could pull into a parking space, one of the vampires waved me forward.

I hesitated, and Izzy groaned, "Follow the bastard. We need to eat him. Eat *from* him. Eat—argh." She groaned against the window.

"You're almost done starving," I promised, pulling up to the guy and stopping when he held out a hand. I noticed an elegant black line around his neck, marking him as mated. "Doesn't his mate mark look like the lady's who took Clem away?"

"Who cares?" Zora muttered.

I bit back a grin.

Them being hangry was kind of hilarious. If they hadn't been underwater for multiple days, I probably would've been tired of it, but I'd barely spoken to them since their hunger set in.

I parked the minivan and unrolled my window. "Blair Davidson?" he asked.

"And my sisters," I agreed.

He lifted a hand to his ear, and I noticed some kind of communication device. "I've got it, cool down," he murmured, then flashed me a small smile. "We'll take your vehicle from here. Go ahead and get out."

"Thanks." I unbuckled, grabbing my sisters' swimsuit coverups off the floor by their feet. "My sisters are starving, so I'm sorry in advance for the barrage of desire you and your team are about to feel. Just try to ignore it."

The guy winced, lifting his hand back to his ear. "Fine," he growled under his breath. "Are you not starving as well, Blair?" he asked, his voice strained.

My forehead creased. "I don't know why it matters to you, but I haven't eaten since they have. I'm just used to being hungry."

And just craving one meal in particular.

I pulled the back door open and dragged Zora out of her seat. Her little red bikini threatened to pop off entirely, so I pulled her floor-length coverup dress over her head.

He relaxed. "Good to know. I'm Egan, by the way. You met my mate, Louise, the last time you were here."

"I thought your mate mark looked like hers." I grabbed Avery's hand to help her out after Zora was leaned up against the door. Her swimsuit was a tight one-piece that covered more skin, but she was dazed too, so I helped her into the plaid button-up she usually threw on with her suit.

Izzy, thankfully, got out of the car herself. She was leaning heavily against the front of the van, though, and her sporty bikini did little to hide her from the view of the now-horny vampires staring hungrily at her.

Yikes.

"I'm going to need some help here," I said apologetically. "Unless you have some guys willing to volunteer to feed us out here."

Murmurs rolled through one of the lines, and Egan winced again, lifting his hand back to his ear and growling something that sounded like, "Shut the fuck up."

He cleared his throat and said, "Hale isn't a fan of that idea. I have a few mated males who can carry your sisters in, if you're comfortable with it. Since you seem alright, it would be better if you walked."

So King Hale was the one on the other end of the line.

Interesting.

Considering how annoyed his right-hand man seemed, it probably wasn't a good omen for us.

"That would be great, thank you," I said anyway. "And I'm fine with walking, but I don't quite have the energy to match vampire speed right now."

I needed to play nice if I was going to try to get information about Damian from Egan, and I did need to try. Though I was surviving, I really did have to feed soon.

"No problem. Vampire speed is prohibited on the path up to the Manor anyway, for security reasons."

"The chase instinct?" I checked.

"Yep."

I nodded, and a few vampires scooped up my sisters. Then, we headed down the path.

A few minutes down the sidewalk, my legs started getting shaky.

I couldn't afford to wait any longer before asking him.

"Do you know any vampires named Damian who live in the city?" I asked Egan, and felt multiple sets of eyes land on me.

He glanced sideways at me. "Why?"

My face warmed a little. "I met him at a nightclub a few weeks ago, and we seemed compatible. Feeding-wise." I added the last bit, just to make it sound less weird. I really needed their help if I was going to find him.

"I can ask around," Egan said vaguely.

My hope dwindled a little.

I was going to have to feed from someone else.

Dammit.

"Thanks." I tried not to get emotional about it. Damian had promised no strings attached, so he probably didn't want to feed me again anyway.

BY THE TIME we reached the Manor, I was leaning heavily on Egan to stay upright. He didn't seem to *want* to help me, but the alternative was to leave me on my ass on the sidewalk. Luckily, he seemed against that.

The vampires marched right past the reception area, and Johnny waved at me. I waved back, and Egan swore under his breath.

"Try not to wave at people," he gritted out.

I flashed him a look. "Why not?"

"Just... never mind." He muttered another curse.

"I could ask someone else to help me," I said.

"No, you can't." He made it sound like it would literally be impossible.

I opened my mouth to do just that, but before I could, we stepped through the doors and into the vampire wing of the Manor.

Insanely tall windows with gleaming white paint on the walls between them filled my view. The stone tile beneath my feet was a charcoal gray so dark it was nearly black, and the glimmering obsidian bits within gave it insane depth.

The furniture we passed was sleek but looked comfortable and worn, and the people in the hallway looked curious enough to make me think their king wasn't a tyrant. If he'd been a dictator, they would've been scared.

And he probably wouldn't have offered to help us.

Then again, he *hadn't* offered to help us. He'd just sort of... summoned us.

Maybe I'd gotten excited too soon. He could very well still turn us away. Or use us the same way Curtis wanted to.

We made it through two endless-feeling hallways and down half of another one before we finally reached a set of huge doors.

That seemed to be a pattern in the Manor, not that it surprised me. A building that gorgeous deserved doors to match.

Two of the guards opened the doors, and Egan all but dragged me inside. Though I was still on my feet, he was holding most of my weight.

My gaze moved over the large, mostly-empty room. Why was it so empty? It looked like a... well, a throne room. But where was the...

My eyes lifted up a few steps, and landed on a gigantic chair that looked like it was worth more than our minivan.

It was definitely a throne room.

My gaze finally landed on the man sitting on the edge of the throne, and I swear, my heart dropped into my stomach.

I knew that dark hair.

That blue, button-up shirt.

Those piercing eyes.

"Damian?" I asked.

"Damian *Hale*," the man on the throne said, his eyes moving slowly down my figure. "I've been looking for you, little siren."

Shit.

Holy shit.

"You had my phone number and left my sisters and I *starving*, so you must not have been looking hard," I finally said.

He chuckled, not looking away from me for a moment. "Egan, clear the room."

"She can hardly stand, Hale. Her sisters passed out in our guards' arms half an hour ago."

His eyes narrowed in on the place Egan was holding me up.

He was on his feet and down the stairs in a heartbeat, and then his arms were on my waist instead of Egan's. "Wake them up and let them choose from the volunteers," he said. "After you clear the room."

Egan grumbled something that sounded like an insult, but he and everyone else filed out.

I looked past him, watching my sisters go. "What are you going to do to them after they feed? You still haven't agreed to protect us."

"I'm getting there."

"I don't see why everyone had to leave for you to—ohh." I groaned into his mouth when his lips captured mine. My magic kicked in immediately, and his emotions flooded me.

Thrill.

Hope.

Desire.

Need.

Desperation.

Fear.

He still tasted amazing.

His magic relaxed me so much I couldn't help but lean in, kissing him deeply as I took more and more.

I pulled away as soon as I could, panting near violently. My fingers were fisted in his shirt again, wrinkling the smooth fabric. His were in my hair.

"At least you managed not to bite me that time," I managed, between deep breaths in.

He chuckled, his voice low and rich. "Don't get used to it."

My forehead creased. "What do you—"

"You need protection," he said. "I need *you*."

I blinked.

"You're my blood mate, Blair. I realized the moment I tasted you in the club, but you left before I could stop you."

I blinked again. "Blood mate, as in..."

"As in, your blood can free me from the desperate hunger I feel constantly as a vampire."

"Oh. That."

"Yes, that."

"What are you proposing, exactly?" I asked, my breathing finally growing steady.

"A mate bond."

My heart nearly stopped. "A *what*?"

"A mate bond, Blair. A marriage. You become my mate, and I protect you and your sisters indefinitely."

Fuck.

"And what if I refuse?"

"Then you have no one to protect you." His words were careful. "And considering the conversation I had with Clementine about exactly who's coming after you, I don't think you have a choice. I'm a fair leader; you can find out that much from my people alone. Curtis and I don't get along."

"So I get to choose between spending my life mated to you, or letting my sister be used by a werewolf who I watched kill a bartender just because she made him angry."

He hesitated just a beat.

It was such a small moment, I thought I might've imagined it.

"Yes," he said.

"Fuck you." I shoved his chest.

He took a step back, but didn't release his hold on my waist.

"I would be trapped here, with you, for the rest of my life."

"You would."

"What about my sisters?"

"They can come and go as they wish, though it will never be completely safe to do so until they've taken mates."

"Will you force or manipulate them into mating with any of your vampires?" I demanded.

"Of course not. If my vampires want siren mates, they need to win them over themselves."

I let out a harsh breath. "Fine. Seeing as I have no other choice, I'll do it. Let's make the vows." I lifted my hand to his throat, but he caught my wrist before I could touch him.

"I'm empathetic enough to your situation to give you some time to consider it. Wearing my mark on your throat willingly is enough for me right now."

"Fine," I repeated, the word coming out clipped. "Do your worst."

He lifted one of his hands to my throat and pressed his palm to my skin lightly. When he leaned in, his lips brushed my ear as he murmured, "You are mine, little siren."

The magic that accompanied the words rolled over my neck and down my chest. My body arched as it slowly spread over the rest of me, drawing me toward the man who'd just marked me as his.

Damian dragged his fingertips lightly over the sensitive skin there, and my hips jerked a little. With a soft growl, he pulled me against him harder.

He inhaled against the side of my throat—then without warning, bit down.

I gasped as the tidal wave of his magic crashed into me, flooding every part of me. Ultimate relaxation melded with hot, intense pleasure, and I grabbed his shirt to anchor myself again.

There was no pain, this time.

Not even a brief moment when he first bit me.

I felt nothing but calm desire, a monstrous swell of need, and the absolute *fire* of knowing I was exactly where I belonged.

In his arms.

Beneath his fangs.

Giving him what he needed.

When he released my neck, dragging his tongue over the mark he'd left on me, I finally started coming back to my senses.

I shoved him away again.

"Fuck you, *Hale*," I snarled.

"If that's an invitation, I accept," he said without batting an eye.

Fury, outrage, and a little bit of sadness burned in my veins. "You can't just bite me whenever you want."

"I can, and I will. And you'll do the same when you need to feed from me."

"Go to hell." My hands trembled, and I turned to storm out of the room.

He caught me before I reached the door, stepping between me and my escape route. His eyes were even brighter than usual, and his shoulders were relaxed in a way that surprised me. "You're sharing my bedroom. Don't try to convince me otherwise."

"Any other helpful advice?" I bit out.

"Don't run from me."

"Wasn't planning on it."

"Our room's on the top floor. Only one of the elevators can get you there. The black one, furthest from the entrance. Level fourteen. The code is 0615. If you're not there when I go to bed, I *will* find you."

I growled, but bit back yet another useless argument.

He had *all* of the power.

I turned to leave again—but he stopped me once more with a hand to my hip. I didn't turn around, but he didn't try to turn me around.

"You'll want to go see the pool soon. The entrance is on the eleventh floor."

When he released my hip, I finally managed to leave the throne room.

As soon as the doors were shut, I collapsed against them, sucking in a breath and squeezing my eyes shut.

What had I just agreed to?

five
BLAIR

"WHAT THE FUCK is on your neck?" Izzy's voice interrupted me from my door-leaning-and-vampire-loathing moment, but I didn't open my eyes. I wasn't ready to deal with my sisters yet. Or myself. Or anything else.

"That's a mate mark," Zora said. "Definitely a mate mark."

"We're not blind," Izzy growled.

Someone smacked her, and she grumbled at them.

"What happened?" Avery asked, and I felt her hand on my shoulder a moment later.

I finally wrestled my eyes open. "I don't know," I said.

They all gave me a look that said I was full of shit.

They were right, too.

So, I sighed. "Let's get away from here. He can probably hear us."

Their attention snapped to the doors behind me, and Clementine looped her arm through mine. "Guess I'm not the only one with a mate mark, though yours looks a lot prettier than mine. Do we need to try to escape the vampires now too?"

"We couldn't escape the vampires if we tried," Zora said, falling into step on my other side and taking my other arm.

"That's a valid point," Izzy grumbled.

"And the vampires are actually really nice," Clem added. "Except maybe Hale. Err, Damian?"

Izzy said, "Can't say I saw that plot twist coming."

"I should've seen it. There were small signs. He ordered the bartender around, and no one batted an eye."

"There were a *lot* of people around him, too," Avery added.

"The seat next to his was empty," I protested.

"I think the vampire king can probably empty a seat when he wants space," she said.

She was right, and we all knew it.

"We can hang out in my room for a bit," Clem said. "Louise told me they would put you guys in the rooms around me. They understand that sirens need each other, at least."

"Damian—Hale—made it very clear that I'll be living in his bedroom," I said. "But at least you guys will be close to each other.

Multiple grimaces came my way.

"It's not too late to go to the werewolves," Clem said quickly, and I heard the guilt in her voice.

"It's *way* too late to go to the werewolves," a feminine voice behind us corrected, and I looked over my shoulder. The woman we'd met before, Egan's mate, was behind us.

Louise, I think her name was.

"Hey, Lou," Clem said with a bright smile, pulling all of us to a stop so the other woman could catch up. "Everyone, this is Louise."

"Didn't you say she's Hale's *sister*?" Zora muttered.

Clem elbowed me in the gut, then whispered, "Oops," when I grunted. She stepped around me to elbow Zora, instead.

"He's not as bad as he might seem," Lou said, her eyes lingering on the marking on my neck. "But he definitely won't let his blood mate go to Curtis. Curt would send her back to him in pieces, just to get a rise out of him."

"*Blood* mate?" Izzy demanded, and all of their eyes were on me again.

"I told you I was craving him," I said weakly.

"It would make sense for you to crave him if you're his blood mate."

"Is there still an *if*?" Izzy asked, hopeful.

"Did he drink from you again?" Louise asked me.

I nodded.

"And did he still want you afterward?"

I grimaced, but nodded again.

"Then no, there's not an *if*."

Izzy sighed in defeat.

Clem recaptured my arm, and we all started moving again. Lou fell into step on the other side of Zora, though Zora kept giving her dirty looks.

She was one of the most loving members of our family. When she was on your side, she would do anything for you. But when she didn't like someone, she would do absolutely anything to make sure they failed.

Avery stepped between Zora and Lou, probably to keep the peace.

"How did the conversation go exactly, when he asked you if he could mark you?" Lou asked curiously.

I felt a few pairs of eyes on us, probably from random vampires in the hallway we were walking through, but I didn't let myself feel self-conscious about the attention. It was Damian's—*Hale's*—fault, not mine.

I scoffed. "He didn't *ask*. He said I could mate with him to guarantee my sisters' safety, or we could leave and let Curtis take us."

Clem sucked in a breath.

Izzy swore.

Avery murmured something to Zora.

Lou sighed. "Lovely. I'll talk to him."

"I don't think talking will help. He made it pretty clear that he's calling the shots, and I'm at his mercy."

"That's not how a mate bond works," Lou argued.

Avery set her hand on Lou's arm. "Tell your brother that."

"I will."

Avery released the other woman as we all kept walking. "Sorry, I didn't mean to grab you. We're touchy."

"I've realized. Clementine has hugged me at least a hundred times since she's been away from you." Lou smiled, making sure we realized it didn't bother her.

"Sirens require snuggling," Clem said with a shrug.

We stopped in front of a door, and Clementine said, "This one's mine."

"The rest of your rooms will be around here too. I actually came to find you for style preferences." She pulled her phone from her pocket. "We decorated the rooms in three different ways, so you can all look through the pictures and decide which one you like the most before we assign the rooms."

My sisters leaned in as she pulled up the photos.

My stomach clenched with too many emotions as they started looking through, slowly.

I took another step back without realizing it.

I... needed to go for a swim.

Yep.

Definitely needed a swim.

Avery's gaze met mine over the phone, and I made the hand motion for water. She nodded, mouthing two words to me before I slipped away.

"Thank you."

My eyes stung as I padded down the hall at human speed. If I had a completed mate bond, the magic of it would suppress everyone else's chase instincts except my mate's, but I didn't.

Thankfully.

But *not* thankfully, when I wanted to move fast.

I FOUND AN ELEVATOR EASILY ENOUGH.

It wasn't the black one, which I'd need to find that night, but an elevator was an elevator.

I stepped inside, and froze just in front of the doors.

They closed behind me, but I barely noticed.

Because there was a mirror on the wall in front of me. A large mirror.

My fingers trembled as I lifted them to the mark around my neck.

It wasn't blocky and hideous, like Clementine's.

It was gorgeous.

The wavy, dark blue band reminded me of water, swirling and twisting lightly. It was darker in some places and lighter in others. Though I didn't want to, I loved it.

The elevator dinged behind me, and the doors opened again.

I jerked away from the mirror, my face flushed as a pair of men stepped inside.

Both of them inhaled, and I saw it in their eyes the moment my magic hit them.

I hadn't fed from Damian long enough to sate myself. I'd pulled away as soon as I'd taken the edge off enough to manage it.

"What floor?" I asked, forcing a smile as I hit the button for the eleventh floor.

"Six," one of the guys managed, snapping out of my pull after a moment.

I hit that button too, and the guy who'd regained control smacked the other one on the arm. When he didn't come to, he punched the side of his throat.

I winced, but the second guy just shook his head. "Shit. Sorry. Not supposed to stare."

"Whoever made up that rule doesn't really understand siren

magic," I said, lifting my eyes to the floor numbers so I could watch us move up.

2...

3...

4...

5...

"It's Hale's rule," the guy finally said.

"Well, he *definitely* doesn't understand siren magic," I murmured.

The elevator dinged as we finally reached the sixth floor.

The guys slipped out without a goodbye, but one of them stuck his hand in the door just before it closed. I flinched at the sudden interruption, and an apologetic look crossed his face.

"I'm not sure if you know this, but one of those rules requires telling him when we can feel your magic so he knows that you're hungry."

"Of course it does. I don't suppose you could keep it to yourself this time?"

He gave me a wry smile. "I would if I could, but I respect Hale too much for that. Enjoy the pool."

He let the elevator close, and I sighed as I watched the numbers rise again.

7...

8...

9...

10...

The doors opened again as we reached the eleventh floor, and I slipped out.

How long would Hale give me to enjoy swimming before he showed up and demanded that I kiss him?

I wasn't even sure I wanted to know.

I could smell chlorine down the hall, and my nose itched.

Gross.

Siren magic naturally cleaned and purified water, so we didn't need chemicals. I'd figure out where their pump room was and make sure to get rid of them while I was there. Or at least write a note to ask someone to get rid of them.

"Why the hell do we need a ten-story pool?" a feminine voice asked, clearly annoyed. "Hale promised us an epic mini-golf course."

"Someone said it has something to do with the sirens we're housing," another woman said.

"Screw the sirens," the first girl grumbled.

"He probably is."

"Not *my* Hale," she argued. "He doesn't even drink blood from the vein. He's not interested in screwing a siren."

My veins disagreed, but I wasn't about to say that aloud.

"He's not yours, Missy."

I stepped into a wide, open room, and my gaze immediately went to the pool.

Holy shit.

It wasn't just a pool... it was a work of art.

Gorgeous, rough stone made it look like a piece of nature had been built in the Manor. There was an arch on one side, and a huge waterfall on another. I saw the water moving in what had to have been a lazy river around the outside, too.

My feet carried me to the edge, and my jaw just about dropped when I realized I could barely see the bottom.

"Here's one of the siren bitches now," the first girl whispered. "I can even feel her slutty magic."

"Want me to make it stronger?" I asked her, without looking up from the water. "I could probably make you take your clothes off if I really tried. Siren hearing is just as good as vampires', by the way."

Missy huffed.

The second woman laughed. "I kind of want to feel it."

"Are you insane?!" Missy protested.

I flashed them a smile, and pushed more of my magic to the surface. Both of them shuddered, and the first girl grabbed the second's arm like she was holding on for dear life.

I released the magic without actually pushing them to do anything. I'd never violate someone like that. Not on purpose, at least. Sometimes, I couldn't control my power at all.

"Damn, that's intense," the second girl said, admiration in her voice.

"Hale is going to hear about this," Missy said, her voice trembling. "We're engaged to be mated. Our parents planned it when we were kids."

"Congratulations." I gave her a warm smile. "And go ahead and tell your *fiancé.* I'm sure you won't be the only person he hears it from." I looked at the second girl. "Any idea where the pump room is?"

"The door's over there. Roscoe runs it. I'll let him know to talk to you about it when I see him. Missy and I are going to head out." She grabbed the other woman's arm, the way Clementine had grabbed mine. Looking at them, I decided there was a good chance they were sisters.

"Thanks."

"Who are you mated to?" she asked, curiosity setting in on her way out.

"You don't want to know." My gaze flicked to Missy, and her sister's eyes widened before she rushed her out the door, mouthing,

"Thank you."

I nodded at her, then headed toward the pump room.

The door was unlocked, and it took all of three seconds for me to realize I was in over my head among the many different buttons and switches.

I saw a pad of paper with a few notes on it though, and grabbed the pen beside it, folding the top page over so I didn't mess up any of their stuff.

I wrote a quick note.

> Roscoe or whoever runs this room,
>
> Please turn everything off if you can get approval from whoever your boss is. The water will flow the way it wants to as long as me or one of my sisters stop by once a week or so, and we'll be here a lot more than that. The magic might wreck your pumps if you leave them on while it's doing its thing.
>
> Our power will remove the chemicals from the water and keep it pure, too. Don't put more chlorine in or Izzy will probably kill you. Chlorine is a bitch to get off a siren's skin. We'll fish out anything that falls to the bottom so you don't have to.
>
> Also, if you throw a rock in while one of us is in the water, we'll know you want us to

come out. Don't ask me why we started that, but it's a thing.
Thanks,
Blair <3

I added a heart at the end, just in case the note sounded harsher than I thought.

After being on the receiving end of Damian's dickishness, I didn't want to put anyone else through that.

I let out a slow breath.

Hale.

His name was Hale.

I needed to accept that he wasn't the guy from the club, and move on. Moving on would make it much easier to wrap my mind around the new, unique situation I'd landed myself in.

Because there was no getting out. I was good and trapped. My other option was Curtis, the bastard who would send me back to *Hale* in *pieces*.

Shudder.

So, my situation was the best of the two options.

At least my sisters were safe and happy.

And I was... well, going to enjoy the most gorgeous pool I'd probably ever see.

So hey, there were *two* perks.

I strode back to the edge of the pool and peeled the over-sized t-shirt I used as a swimsuit coverup over my head. It fell to the floor as I dove in.

The water engulfed me, and I inhaled deeply.

Heaven.

I was in heaven.

...even if it smelled and tasted like chlorine.

six

DAMIAN

I PACED MY OFFICE, shoving a hand through my hair. The gel had dried it in weird shapes because of the repetitive motion, but I didn't give a damn.

It was taking everything I had not to track my female down.

She was hungry—I'd heard as much from two different sources.

My little siren hadn't taken enough from me.

And my bloodlust was already starting to set in again. I should've fed on her longer, but I'd been afraid to hurt her.

She couldn't make that excuse.

That said, I knew I was on thin ice with her.

Hell, I was on *broken* ice with her.

I'd been afraid to lose her, and I'd been a fucking moron because of it. Threatening her clearly wasn't the way to go.

Not only because she'd looked at me like I was a monster afterward, but because of the way it made me feel like one.

Typically, I could do whatever I needed to without feeling a thing. I had to be able to compartmentalize that way, considering how many vampires I had relying on me.

But with her, I couldn't do it.

Trying had been a mistake.

One I wasn't sure how to correct.

Especially when she wanted to do things I couldn't handle —like letting her walk around my Manor while her magic was drawing everyone to her side.

Someone tried to open my office's locked door, and I bit back a curse.

If it was another vampire coming by to say they'd lusted after my mate, someone was going to lose their head.

The doorknob moved again, and I relaxed when it opened up.

Only two people had keys.

Louise, and Egan.

I could handle them.

I prepared for a lecture from Louise, but let out a pent-up breath when Egan was the one who stepped inside and relocked the door behind him.

The bastard didn't say a word as he plopped down in a chair, watching me.

"What?" I grumbled

"Nothing. I'm waiting to hear what happened after you made me clear the room."

I let out a rough breath. "I'm sorry. I couldn't think straight. Still can't, to be honest."

"Almost like you could feel your mate's magic actively pulling other males in to fuck her?" Egan drawled.

A harsh laugh escaped me. "Yeah, almost like that."

He chuckled. "Their magic packs a punch. Makes me really damn glad I've got a bond that stops it from touching me."

"Can't say I blame you for that." I sat down in my chair, leaning back against the thick cushion. "I handled it wrong."

"Is there a right way to handle this situation?"

"There's got to be a better one than mine."

"What happened?"

I grimaced, and admitted to the ultimatum I'd given her. The one I absolutely wouldn't have been able to go through with.

I'd sooner chain her hungry little ass to my side and watch the hoards of men come on to her for the rest of our lives than turn her or her family over to Curtis.

I filled Egan in on everything else that had gone down, too.

"I should've come up with something better," I grumbled.

Egan laughed. "What was the alternative? You wouldn't have stayed sane if that woman walked out of the room without drinking from you and feeding you. If she'd left without a mate mark, the first person to lust after her would've died."

"If I'd just come out and told her—"

"She's a siren who spent her entire life hiding to avoid a mate bond. She wouldn't have willingly promised herself to you just to help you avoid killing your own people because of mating lunacy," he said bluntly.

I grimaced.

He was right—a logical explanation wouldn't have been enough.

"What you said wasn't what she wanted to hear, but it was the truth. If she's not in your bed, you won't be able to stop yourself from hunting her down any more than another mated male would. Myself included. Her lust will set you off. She needs to sate herself on you, and you need to sate yourself on her."

"How the fuck am I going to make her fall in love with me, then?"

Egan grinned. "You don't *make* your mate fall in love with you. You stick around and tell her the truth, and eventually she realizes she can't live without your stubborn ass anymore than you can live without hers."

I barked out a laugh. "Romantic."

"Romance is a lie. Real love is strong and determined. It's a white-knuckled hold that you refuse to release, no matter how hard things get. It can be stubborn and bloody, and sometimes it hurts—but it's as good as you make it. And you can make it really fucking good."

I ran a hand through my hair. "I just need to see her."

"Then go find her. She probably needs to see you too."

"And if she doesn't?"

"Stick around and bug her. Eventually, she'll realize she'd rather spend her whole life being bugged by you than alone."

"Sounds like wishful thinking."

"I would think you've had enough loneliness in your life to understand."

He was right.

It used to feel good to wake up alone. To have a peaceful life full of things I enjoyed.

But the novelty had faded ages ago.

And as it did, I would've killed to have someone there to mess up the perfection. To bring things they loved. To make some noise.

"Is that what worked with Lou?"

He barked out a laugh. "You don't want to know how well."

"Probably true." I stretched my legs out beneath the desk. "Alright, I'm going to find her. But if it blows up in my face, you're the one who has to wipe away my tears."

He snorted. "Get out of here."

I laughed. "Tell Lou I'm working on her mountain of paperwork. And tell her not to hate me for pissing off the sirens. I can tell she has a soft spot for them."

He saluted me. "Yes sir."

I rolled my eyes, and he grinned.

BLAIR

I'D BEEN LYING on the bottom of the pool, processing the emotions of the day for what felt like a lifetime when the first shoe sunk down beside me.

My eyes followed it past the gorgeous rock formations and jewel-inlaid walls to the floor of the pool.

It was a man's dress shoe.

How had someone dropped their shoe while walking next to a pool? That kind of clumsiness shouldn't have existed among vampires.

A minute went by before another shoe followed.

That one landed on my boob.

I made a noise of indignation.

I could almost believe one shoe was an accident, but two?

No male vampire would *accidentally* drop both of their shoes into a pool.

Someone was trying to summon me.

I couldn't prevent the wave of excitement—and dread—when I realized there was only one man who would summon me like that.

Hale.

With all the fury of a pissed-off woman, I grabbed both of the shoes and swam hard to the surface, throwing both shoes out of the water first.

"What kind of asshole summons a woman with his shoes?" I demanded, lifting myself smoothly out of the water. Magic was probably radiating off me, but I didn't care. It wasn't like Hale hadn't felt it before.

I—

"Sorry," an unfamiliar man apologized, and my gaze jerked upward.

Oh, shit.

He was *not* Hale.

Very much not Hale.

And I'd thrown shoes at him.

"I'm sorry," I said quickly. "I thought you were Hale."

"It's fine. Getting hit in the face with a shoe is a good way to keep a guy on his toes," the man said, his gaze glued to my breasts.

I sighed inwardly, and tried to pull my magic back. I hadn't had anywhere near enough from Hale, and I was physically hungry on top of that, so my control was basically nonexistent.

"You should throw another shoe at me. Maybe it will make it easier to stop staring at you?" he mumbled.

I laughed, grabbing the shoe and tossing it at him.

He made a noise of complaint. "Useless. Throw it like I'm Hale again."

"Do *what* like you're me?" the growl was the only warning before Hale himself sped into the room, stopping beside the stranger.

"She threw a shoe at me," he explained quickly, fighting desperately to look away from me. "She thought I was you. I used it to get her attention while she was underwater, because we had no rocks."

I stood smoothly, crossing the room so I could grab my oversized t-shirt off the floor. Water rolled down my body, and I fought the urge to scratch at the layer of glitter the chlorine had formed over my skin.

Scientifically, I didn't think it made a shred of sense for chlorine to create glitter. But siren magic didn't make sense, so that was that.

"Why are you sparkling?" Hale asked me, his eyes now glued to me too.

"Chlorine and siren magic don't mix well." I shook my arm, and a small amount of glitter fell from my skin. Most of it wouldn't come off until I scrubbed like hell. Even then, a lot of it would simply refuse to budge for a few days. That was fine, though. Sirens made good disco balls.

"That's in the note, but I didn't think it would make glitter... fascinating." The new guy started to flip to a new page, to make notes, but Hale pulled the notepad out of his hand and scanned the words I'd written.

"Why are you signing a note with a heart for a guy who isn't your mate?" he growled at me.

"Do you even have a normal voice? All you do is growl at me." I wrung my hair out, watching glitter-water pool beneath it. "Hearts make things nicer. They don't have to be romantic. Everyone knows that."

The perplexed expressions on their faces told me that everyone, in fact, did not know that.

"Never mind. Do you guys have a kitchen here or something? I need to eat before I cause an orgy to break out."

I meant it as a joke, but the look on Hale's face told me he would absolutely murder everyone involved if that occurred.

"That was supposed to be funny. It's never happened before, and I don't think it's actually possible, based on the way my magic works. Breathe, Hale. I was just saying that I'm hungry."

"I'll feed you," the new guy blurted out, then cringed when Hale snarled at him. "I don't know why I said that. He'll feed you. Not me. I have a girlfriend."

"It's my magic's fault. I can't control it right now," I apologized. "I can explain to your girlfriend if she's worried."

"You met her already. She understands, and she warned me," he admitted, his face red.

"Oh, your girlfriend is his fiancé's sister?" I gestured to Hale, whose forehead creased.

"Yeah, I'm Roscoe." He lowered his voice and whispered to Hale, "Missy still tells people you're engaged."

Annoyance filled his expression. "How many fucking times do I have to have that conversation?" he pulled his phone out, and his fingers flew across the screen.

"Even that won't stop her," Roscoe warned, reading over his shoulder.

Hale paused, and considered it.

A wicked gleam filled his eyes, and he lifted his phone toward me.

"What are you doing?" I asked warily.

I heard what sounded like a camera taking a picture.

"That picture will turn people on," Roscoe said matter-of-factly.

"Her existence turns them on." He typed something out as I hurried across the room.

"Oh, that's good," Roscoe said, approving of the message before I heard the sound of it being sent.

"What did you do, Hale?" I demanded.

"I told you to call me Damian, little siren."

"Damian is the name of someone who wouldn't force me into mating with him."

"I stopped you from reciprocating the bond, didn't I?"

The question caught me off guard, but I distracted myself by taking his phone and reading his text instead of answering.

The group chat's label said: VAMP MANOR HOMIES.

"Homies?" I drawled.

"Someone else made the group. No one will tell me who," he grumbled.

My eyes nearly bulged when I saw a picture of myself in my wet shirt, my hair dripping as the fabric clung to my curves and showed off the glitter on my skin.

Below it, he'd written out a message.

HALE

Everyone, this is my mate, Blair. Apparently sirens can be glittery. I'll have a good fucking time licking her clean tonight. Anyone who touches her loses a hand.

"What's wrong with you?" I hissed. "You are not licking *any part of me* tonight."

"The impact is the same anyway," Roscoe explained. "He just marked you as his in every way to the whole Manor, and everyone else they know. Even Missy won't be able to argue with that declaration."

"He just made me even more of a target than I already am," I protested.

"Nah, the only ones brave enough to target Hale's mate are the other kings," Roscoe said.

"How many times do I have to say we're not kings?" Hale grumbled.

My stomach growled, and both mens' eyes dilated as my magic flared.

Hale grabbed me by the waist. "Do whatever she wants to the pool. It's hers."

Despite the possessive growl in his voice, the words were a turn-on. A serious turn-on.

"You should add that to the message," Roscoe called behind her. "So people stop wondering why you put this in instead of the mini-golf course we voted for."

"There was supposed to be a mini-golf course?" I yelled over Hale's shoulder, as he turned the corner.

"An epic one!" Roscoe shouted back.

"Why'd you kill the mini-golf course? Everyone likes mini-golf," I said, trying to adjust my position on his shoulder so my ribs wouldn't hurt so bad.

"My mate's a siren. Fuck mini-golf."

"You built a pool for me? You didn't even know me until today!"

"I told you, I was looking for you. I had to do it quietly, or the whole city would realize there was an unmated siren wandering around. I knew you were mine the moment I tasted your blood."

My forehead creased. "Not the moment you felt my magic?"

He turned down a hallway and strode over toward a shiny, black elevator. It had to be the one he'd mentioned would take us to our room.

"Of course not. Your magic feels nice, but I don't care about that any more than I care about the damn golf course."

"So you *don't* want me because I'm a siren?"

"No. My life would be much easier right now if you were a raccoon shifter."

I choked out a laugh. "Somehow, that's the most romantic thing you've ever said to me."

"Romance is bullshit."

"Whatever you say." I peeled a strip of wet hair off my face as he hit the button to call the elevator. "I don't think this is the way to the food."

"No, but I'm not taking you to dinner wearing this. I need to buy you a wetsuit or something."

"A *wetsuit?*" I made a face. "I'm a siren, Hale. We're supposed to swim naked and free, so we can feel the water on our bare breasts. Or something like that, anyway. This bikini is as close to a wetsuit as you're getting me."

"We can argue about that later."

"We most certainly can*not*. I'm done arguing about my swimwear."

"Argue with me about my name, then."

That was a good transition. A really good transition.

The elevator dinged, and he stepped inside, typing the code he'd given me.

0615.

June 15th.

A date from a few weeks ago.

I went back mentally, and frowned a little when I realized it was the day we'd met in the nightclub.

Why had he picked that?

We weren't close enough to ask, but maybe at some point I would.

"Why does what I call you matter that much?" I asked.

"I started going by Hale to distance myself from the guy I was before I took over the vampire wing of the Manor.

You're my mate. I don't want to be that version of myself with you."

The admission—and the vulnerability—made my stomach tighten. "You can't tell me things like that after forcing me to wear your mate mark and threatening to put me in a wetsuit," I finally said.

"Sure I can."

"What am I supposed to think in this situation?" I asked him, frustration swelling within me. "I don't want a mate, okay? I never have. My mom's mate loved her so much that he killed the women that were her family, and accidentally killed her too. Mate bonds are bullshit. *Love* is bullshit. I don't want anything to do with any of it."

"That sounds like psychosis, not love." The elevator dinged on our floor. "And I didn't propose love. I proposed a mate bond that will mutually benefit both of us. I need your blood to sate my bloodlust. You need my emotions so you don't have to starve or kiss strangers anymore. It's a win-win situation."

"One you forced me into," I reminded him.

"I gave you a choice. You picked the most reasonable option."

"Oh, fuck off," I growled, trying to see his room.

There were few things the myths got right about vampires, but I knew the coffin thing was one of them. Vampires usually slept in coffins. They weren't your typical horror-movie coffin, but a mattress with a lid of sorts that just went over the top when you were ready to sleep.

I knew that, because...

Well, because sirens are basically emotional vampires.

We're closely related enough to them that we also sleep in coffins.

It sounds weird, but it's cozy as fuck.

And we don't call them coffins—we just call them canopy beds. With canopies that move down and become snuggly forts.

He draped me over the edge of the mattress, then leaned over me with a gleam in his eyes. "Agree to wear a coat and snow pants to dinner, and I'll agree to fuck off."

I scowled. "I'm not doing that."

"Then neither am I. Now, are you going to change before you kiss me, or after?"

"I don't have any clothes here."

"You'll wear mine. We can get yours tomorrow."

"I don't want your security team knowing where my house is," I countered.

"I wasn't going to *bring* my security team. Just you, and me. And any of your sisters who want to come, minus Clementine."

"Has Curtis tried to take her from you yet?" I asked, momentarily distracted from how much I disliked him.

"No. Breaking into my wing of the Manor would be an act of war, and even Curtis is smart enough not to risk that. No one likes him enough to fight with him."

"No one, meaning..."

"None of the other guys."

"The other *kings*?"

"Leaders," he amended. "We're not kings."

"You keep saying that, but it keeps being untrue."

He rolled his eyes.

"You're friends with the other *leaders*?"

"Yeah. They're assholes, but it comes with the territory."

"Which ones could beat you in a fight?"

"On a good day, none of them."

"And on a bad day?"

"Any of them," he admitted. "We're evenly matched, as annoying as it is. After you seal your side of the mate bond, I'll introduce you to them."

"Not before?"

His eyes darkened. "Not a fucking chance. Some of those broody bastards could use a siren in their lives, and they can't have you. Or your sisters."

"You're possessive of my sisters now, too?" I asked, lifting an eyebrow.

"You're a packaged deal."

"That's true." I ran a hand through my hair. "We're already here, so I might as well kiss you."

"Every man dreams of being kissed by a woman this reluctant," he drawled.

I smiled. "We were never about lust, Damian."

I could see the appreciation in his eyes as he lowered his lips to my throat and brushed them lightly over the band around my neck. "Maybe *you* weren't."

"You did *not* want me in that nightclub."

He barked out a laugh. "Like hell I didn't." His teeth slid into my throat, and I gasped, arching my back. My legs wrapped around his hips as his magic relaxed me and made me want him desperately, at the same time.

"You already drank from me today," I breathed, my entire body flushed.

"Not enough," he said against my throat.

"Are you sure it's not just my magic?" I moaned, threading my fingers through his hair and pulling him against me harder. His teeth sank in deeper, and I cried out, right on the edge of an orgasm.

Just before I could finish, he released me with a kiss to my throat and a swipe of his tongue. His bites seemed to heal instantly, unlike most of my injuries. I healed a lot faster than a human, but it was nowhere near instant most of the time. "Your magic makes me want to fuck you, not bite you, little siren. And bloodlust is unmistakable."

"What does it feel like?" I whispered, my chest rising and falling quickly as pain tightened my abdomen.

I needed a release, badly.

And I still hadn't managed to peel my legs off his waist.

His eyes clouded a little. "Like you're going to die if you don't drink blood. But the more you drink, the more you need. It's an endless cycle."

"How does my blood make you feel?"

"Free." The word was simple, but enough to make my chest ache.

I could understand that desire.

That need.

Hell, I wanted it myself.

He kissed my throat again. "Tastes fucking good, though."

He was trying to lighten the mood, and I appreciated that. But there were bigger, more important things to deal with.

"You're never going to let me walk away, are you?" I asked quietly, my hand still buried in his hair though my grip wasn't as tight.

"Even if I wanted to, I couldn't." The admission was raw, and honest.

"*Do* you want to?"

"No."

I tightened my grip on his hair. "Sealing the bond will let me drink your emotions without kissing you. It's freedom for me, too. More freedom than I have right now, at least."

Surprise flickered in his eyes. "You don't need to—"

I lifted my free hand to his throat, wrapping it around his like he had mine, and said, "You are mine, Damian."

The magic that blossomed between us was fierce enough to rip the breath right out of my lungs. His mouth was on mine before the power faded, both his hands on my ass as he lifted me higher and pressed against me harder.

I drank his emotions, taking what I needed and so, so much more.

"Fuck me," I commanded, wildly sated and desperately horny when I finally released his mouth.

He shoved my swim bottoms aside and filled me with his fingers a heartbeat later, making me cry out with pleasure.

His thumb found my clit, and it only took one rough brush against it to shatter me.

I panted hard as I came down from the high, his hot gaze burning into me and his thumb still stroking my clit.

"That was—" I cut myself off, with no idea how to finish it. "We can—"

"You're hungry. The emotions of the mate bond are still running high. I'm not taking you for the first time when there's a chance you might regret it."

"You say that like it'll happen more than once."

His lips curved upward, his smile wicked. "The bond will prevent you from wanting anyone but me, little siren. Eventually, you'll get desperate enough to fuck me. And after you've had me, you'll never be done with me."

"That sounds like a challenge," I tossed back.

"No, it's a promise." He leaned down to kiss my throat, and my chest constricted. "You want to get off again before I pull out?"

"Yes." The whispered admission escaped me before I could stop myself.

"Needy little thing." His words were playful. But the way he ran his thumb over my clit was *anything* but that.

I moaned, "If you fuck Missy with these fingers, I'll rip your cock off."

"You're mine, remember? If I want a sexy little female to fill, I have this one."

"Fuck, I hate you."

"Hate is a hell of a lot like love, don't you think?"

I gasped when he ground his hand against my clit, making my hips rock harder. "Shut up and get me off, Damian."

He chuckled, his voice low and rich. "I'm going to jerk off to those words tonight."

"Don't even think about it."

"I'd like to see you stop me. Now, quit talking and come for me, little siren."

I laughed breathlessly—then cried out when he worked me harder, until I was clenching around him as I lost control completely.

He kissed my throat again, straightening as he continued to tease my clit lightly while I came down from my high. Then, he kissed my knee.

"There's glitter on your lips," I said, my breathing still unsteady.

He licked my knee. "Now it's on my tongue, too."

"You really do want people to think you went down on me."

"I want people to know that you're taken." He dragged his thumb lightly over my clit, making my hips jerk. "And is this really that different from going down on you?"

No, it wasn't.

"Your blush answers that question for me." He licked my other knee, then gave my clit one last stroke before he slid his hand out slowly.

My core clenched around nothing, my body already missing him the moment he was gone.

He lifted his hand to his lips and licked my pleasure off his fingers, glitter and all. My breathing picked up again.

I should've asked for three orgasms.

"This doesn't change anything," I said. "I still think you're an asshole, and I still don't want a mate."

His gaze was on me as he finished licking his fingers clean and ran them down the inside of my thigh. "I don't expect anything to change, but this is permanent, little siren." He lifted his slick fingers to the mark I'd put on his throat. "You belong to me."

"And *you* belong to *me*," I said.

"That's right. If you hear anyone say otherwise, you make that clear."

"When was the last time you had sex with Missy? I feel like that's an important thing to consider, here."

"I've never had sex with her."

I narrowed my eyes at him.

"I won't ever lie to you. And you already don't like me, Blair. I have no reason to tell you anything but the truth."

That... was valid logic, actually.

His answer wouldn't have changed my opinion of him, even if he said he screwed her that morning.

"Why is she so insistent, then?"

"Our parents arranged a marriage when we were kids. I refused as a teenager, and they shredded the contract. Missy keeps bringing it up anyway."

"Are your parents still alive?"

"No, they passed away fifty years ago now."

I winced. "I don't think I want to know how old you are."

He chuckled. "Probably not."

My stomach rumbled again, and he stood up. Those gorgeous blue eyes met mine, and the look in them was genuine. "I'm sorry about your parents."

"It was a long time ago."

"Time doesn't erase pain."

"Maybe not." He squeezed my knee. The one he'd licked, repeatedly. "I'll grab you some of my clothes to wear."

With that, he strode into the closet, his erection raging through his jeans.

"You have glitter in your hair," I called out behind him. "And on your hands.

"I'd like to have it on my cock, too," he called back, and I laughed.

"Better get rubbing, then."

His snort made me warm.

He was an asshole... but maybe we could figure out a way to be friends, during the moments I didn't hate him.

eight

BLAIR

MY SISTERS WERE CHATTING up a storm with a small group of vampires who sat around them when we made it down to the dining room.

At least, some of them were.

Okay, fine, *Clementine* was.

Zora looked annoyed.

Izzy was sleeping, with her head on the table and her plate cleared in front of her.

Avery was nodding, but she looked severely uncomfortable in the conversation. Knowing her, she just didn't want to hurt anyone's feelings by shutting it down.

None of us were used to talking with people outside our family in any sort of capacity unless it involved a nightclub. Even then, it was only to keep us alive.

Learning how to live in the Manor, surrounded by vampires, was going to take some serious adjustment.

The vampires served their meals restaurant-style, but there were only two food options, to simplify things. Everyone who lived in the Manor had a job, and the dining room made up a fair number of those. Damian had explained that to me on our way down from our room.

We put in orders on our phones after we arrived, then headed over to my sisters.

Two of the vampires sitting at their table excused themselves when they saw me and Damian coming. They were doing it to make space for us, but considering the absolute misery in Avery's eyes, it wouldn't surprise me in the slightest if they just wanted to get out of the conversation.

"Hey," she murmured, when we sat down.

"Nice outfit," Zora said with a snort. "Looks like you had a run-in with some chlorine, too."

"I am the epitome of fashion," I said, rolling up the sleeves of my six-sizes-too-big long-sleeved shirt yet again. The pants were only staying on my waist because Damian had tied a knot in the waistband itself. "And the glitter was worth it. You need to see the pool here. It's insane."

"How long until the chlorine's gone?" Zora checked.

I shrugged, looking at Damian. He shrugged too.

She made a face. "I'll try to suffer without it for a few days. Your magic will purify it out eventually."

"I'll brave the glitter with you," Clementine said cheerfully. "Glitter's going to become all the rage in the Manor for the next few weeks."

She held her phone out to Zora, whose eyebrows lifted when she saw the picture of me that Damian had sent.

I sighed.

She handed it over to Avery, who bit back a smile.

"So, Hale," Zora said, studying the guy with new eyes. She'd undoubtedly seen his message underneath the picture. "Are we going to bring up the matching mate marks? Because that seems like something worth bringing up, don't you think?"

"Run," Avery murmured to him, and Damian snorted.

"I think they're enough of a statement on their own, don't you?" he asked.

"Sure, if the statement you want to make is, *I forced a siren to mate with me.*"

Avery put her face in her hands.

Clementine sighed.

"That *is* what happened, isn't it?" Zora prodded.

Damian's nostrils flared, but he looked at me.

He wanted my permission before going toe-to-toe with my sister. And I would give it to him... but the dining room had quieted around us.

People were watching.

This conversation was important. Not for my sisters, or for me, but for the stability of the Manor. Considering how many vampires it housed, and the fact that it was protecting us too, that stability was important.

"We had fun. Look at the glitter in his hair. It's even in the scruff on his face," I pointed out, reaching up to ruffle his hair just so she could see more of it. "He actually told me not to seal the bond until I was ready, but I wanted to be able to drink his emotions without kissing him. So, I sealed it. Feel free to question him, but don't go accusing him of hurting me or taking my freedom. If that happened, I'd kill him myself."

Normal discussion slowly resumed around the room, and I hoped I'd avoided any sort of negative outcome with my answer.

He squeezed my thigh lightly, but released it when our plates arrived.

"How big is the pool, exactly?" Avery asked.

"*Huge*," Clementine said, her eyes bright. "But Hale hasn't let anyone swim in it until today, so I've only looked at it. They built that thing insanely fast."

I frowned.

The rest of my sisters shot him inquisitive looks.

"I built the pool for Blair. I wasn't going to open it until she got here," he said simply. "And the crew only finished it a few days ago, so it wasn't a big deal to make everyone swim in the other pool."

I whipped my head around to face him. "There's *another* pool?"

"Yes."

I looked at Clementine.

"It's beautiful," she assured me. "Gorgeous blue tile. Massive dive tank. Great lap area." She made an okay sign with her fingers and kissed it, making Zora snort.

"You're ridiculous," Zora said, though the words were playful.

"I know." Clem leaned her head against Zora's shoulder.

"Now I feel like I'm missing out," Avery teased me.

"We'll go pool-hopping tomorrow," I promised.

"In that wetsuit we talked about, I hope," Damian drawled.

"Bring that up again and I'm swimming in the nude," I warned.

He mimed zipping his lips and throwing the key away, earning laughs around the table.

"I feel like there's a story behind this," Clementine said.

I leaned over the table. "It started with a shoe hitting me in the boob..."

By the time I was done, all of my awake sisters were laughing. Even Zora seemed to have warmed to Damian a little.

And while my goal wasn't to make them like him, I was glad I wasn't arguing about his virtue anymore.

DAMIAN and I walked back to the elevator together, slipping back into our room. The way I ditched his sweats on the floor and climbed into our bed felt oddly intimate, even though he was in the shower while I did.

My heart beat faster than usual as I tried to get comfortable beneath the blankets. I was used to sleeping with the bed's canopy lowered over me, and blamed my discomfort on that as I adjusted the pillows for the fifth time.

But given our conversation earlier, I knew exactly what he was doing in the shower.

The only thing separating us was an archway and a few feet in both directions. If I looked through the arch, I would see him.

After a few more minutes, I angled myself away from him and padded over to a chair in the corner of the room, grabbing one of the extra pillows I'd seen. Finally, I let myself take the room in.

The floors were rustic-looking wood. The walls were a shade of deep green that reminded me of the forest, but somehow still felt neutral. All of the art was landscapes, and I itched to look closer at them.

I wouldn't have expected to find the large, open, dark space comfortable, but I did. Something about it just felt like home.

Which was ridiculous, considering that my home didn't have dark walls or wood floors.

I couldn't stop myself from feeling that, though.

And even if I could've, what was the point? The Manor was my new home, even if it hadn't been my first choice. Our options were to integrate into vampire society or let Curtis use and abuse us, so we needed to fight like hell for the former.

When I turned to walk back to the bed, I couldn't get my feet to move.

My eyes had caught on the man in the shower—the stunningly beautiful man. The fancy dark tile within only served to make him stand out more as he stood with a palm on the wall and stroked his cock with his other hand.

Fire rolled through my veins.

I wanted him.

I really, really wanted him.

His ass was two perfect bubbles, his dark hair plastered to his skin instead of perfectly done, and his cock...

Well, he was proportional.

And the man was freaking huge.

His body shuddered, and mine tensed as I watched him come all over the shower wall.

It was intimate.

Way too intimate.

I forced myself to hurry back to the bed, my entire body clenched with how attracted to him I was.

That had to be because of our mate bond, didn't it?

Settling back into bed, I set my second pillow down vertically in the middle of the mattress, then snuggled up against the divider I'd created.

There.

Now, I wouldn't be tempted to wrap myself around Damian's perfect body.

A few minutes later, the man came strolling through the arch that led into the bathroom. He smelled amazing, but I wasn't about to say that.

Closing my eyes, I tried to act like I was asleep, so he wouldn't realize what I'd seen.

I didn't hear him put clothes on.

Which was bad news for my logical self, and great news for my outrageously horny side.

"The smell of your desire is so fucking delicious," he murmured, and I heard him tuck himself into bed. "You watched me, didn't you?"

"I may have accidentally caught a glimpse while I was looking for another pillow," I said into my divider.

"Good. All I could think about was you."

My body flushed further. "I don't think this shared bedroom thing is going to work. I need more space. This is way too intense."

"You can move to another room, but I'll follow you there. You belong to me. I'm not letting you sleep away from me."

"Why not?"

"Because if I can't see you, I have no idea who you're with." The words were blunt, but not entirely surprising.

"You should be able to trust me, if we're going to share our lives like this."

"Trust takes time."

"Love does too. And I'd like to avoid that, at all costs."

"Don't fall in love with me, then." He said the words casually, like I was able to prevent something very natural.

"If you would wear clothes to bed, or at least let me have my own mattress, that would be easier," I tossed back.

He chuckled. "No."

"You're infuriating," I grumbled.

"I'm aware." He hit the button to lower the canopy over us, and some part of me immediately settled as darkness wrapped around us.

"Don't move this pillow out from between us," I whispered.

"I won't. Feel free to climb over it and have your way with me if you get horny. I'll sacrifice sleep for sex at any hour."

I scowled. "Of course you will."

"I'm not kidding. Sit on my face, climb on my cock... I have no limits."

"Go to sleep, asshole." I swatted at him, and he chuckled again.

"Goodnight, little siren.

I snuggled my pillow a little tighter, praying I wouldn't climb over it in my sleep. I needed to channel the humans' vampire legends and sleep like the dead.

Hell, maybe I needed to invest in a few wooden stakes and some garlic, too.

It wouldn't work... but it just might be my best shot at stopping myself from catching feelings for the big, gorgeous bastard.

DAMIAN

I WOKE UP BEFORE BLAIR, and let myself take her in for a few minutes before I moved.

Unfortunately, she was still clinging to that damn pillow, snuggled up like it was her mate instead of me.

Winning her over would take time.

I was going to have to be patient.

Patience just fucking sucked.

I hit the button to raise the canopy enough to roll out of bed, then lowered it for her again. She could sleep in, but I had work to do. Way too much work. My month-long tournament ensured that.

I'd gone through the highest priority portion of Louise's paperwork mountain and made plans to handle the reasonable requests we had received. Most of them were from smaller vampire clans around the country who needed help, training, a protective escort to Mistwood, or money.

Usually money.

I had to connect those clans with the people in charge of our finances. When they set up meetings, they'd set them up with every individual clan member, and I'd be asked to join most of them.

It was painfully boring, every time.

But they needed me, so I didn't turn them down. I was their leader for a reason.

I got dressed and rummaged around in the library portion of our room for a piece of paper, scribbling out a quick note.

> *Little Siren,*
> *I'll be working in my office until you're ready to go pick up your things. Try to leave without me and I'll chain you to my side. Your sisters are invited too, if they want to come. I can bring extra vampires to pack their things if they'd rather.*
> *Damian <3*

The heart was added after a moment's pause. She'd said she liked hearts the day before, and I needed to use every small advantage she gave me when the woman despised me like she did.

I grabbed a bit of tape and stuck the note on the elevator's frame so she wouldn't miss it. Then, I called the elevator and headed out.

Work made the time pass quickly. I finally looked away from my computer's screen when my office doorknob jiggled a little before noon.

"Why did you lock the door?" Blair called out from the other side. Something within me eased with her presence.

I hadn't gotten messages from anyone who'd felt her magic yet, but I'd checked my phone more than a handful of times just to make sure I hadn't missed anything.

Part of me itched to get one, just so I had an excuse to track her down.

I crossed the room quickly, unlocking and opening the door without pause.

The sight of her alone made me let out a breath I hadn't realized I was holding.

She was still wearing my long-sleeved tee, at least. It fell to her knees, so it covered enough of her that I wasn't itching to throw her in a room and lock her away from the rest of my vampires. Her hair was a mess, and I suppressed the urge to run my fingers through it. Not to smooth it—just to feel it.

I was fucking obsessed.

There was still glitter all over her, but somehow, that made me want her even more.

"People stop by randomly. I like knowing they can't get in unless I let them. I'll get you a key," I said.

"It's fine, I won't be distracting you often." She glanced around my office without stepping inside, then met my gaze again. "Ready to go?"

"Yeah, just give me a minute to finish this last email."

Blair nodded, leaning against the doorway while I went back to my seat and resumed typing. Vampire speed was useful, but when it came to computer work, it didn't really have a place. My mind could only move so fast, so typing speed had to match my thoughts.

After hitting the button to send it, I finally shut it off and made my way back to her.

"All of my sisters are coming," she said as I crossed the room. "Except Clementine, of course."

"The more the merrier." I locked the door before closing it behind us, and tucked my hands in my pockets as we headed for the elevator just so I wouldn't be tempted to take her hand.

"Where do you want me to tell them to meet us?"

"The first level of the parking garage. The button is LL1."

"Got it." She sent them a message. "Let's just take our van."

"There are five of you. I have to imagine you need more things than we can fit in a minivan," I said.

She reluctantly agreed.

"I have a moving truck. We'll take that."

"You own your own moving truck?" The look she gave me told me she thought I was insane.

"Technically, the vampire portion of the Manor owns it."

"And you own the Manor." She nodded. "Alright, I get it. I guess you have to help people move pretty often."

I nodded.

We stepped into the elevator, and she hit the button to send it down.

"You signed your note with a heart this morning," she said as it descended.

"You like hearts."

She hesitated, like she wanted to say something else. Instead, she changed gears. "I'll need your phone number at some point."

"You already have it. I'm the one who called you yesterday. I needed to hear your voice, to be sure it was you."

Her forehead creased.

She went to her calls and hit the button to send me a message.

BLAIR

Hi

I pulled my phone from my pocket and showed her the screen so she could see that it was, in fact, my number.

The elevator landed, and we stepped into the parking garage. I spoke with the attendant for a few minutes while we waited for her sisters, and when the three of them had arrived, we headed out.

There weren't enough seats in the truck, so they all climbed into their van, leaving me to drive the obnoxiously large vehicle alone. Because they didn't want to give me the address, I reluctantly agreed just to follow them there.

I'd be able to find it again if I wanted to, so I thought that was pointless. But if that made them feel better, I'd keep my mouth shut.

When we arrived, I took in the sight of their home. It looked more like an industrial building than a house, made entirely out of cement and with a few large garage doors along the length of it.

No wonder they'd stayed hidden for so long.

The girls chatted like normal as they headed towards one of the doors, but I caught a whiff of something strange as we approached.

My forehead creased as I tried to place it.

It almost smelled like...

Dogs.

Realization crashed into me as the door started to rise.

Snarling, I threw myself in front of the sirens just as a group of massive wolves came barreling toward us. Werewolves were much larger than typical wolves—their heads nearly reached mine.

I'd fought them enough times not to give a damn about their size. I was far faster and stronger than a normal vampire when I needed to be, and even the slowest vamp could take down a wolf if they knew what they were doing.

Assuming the wolf wasn't with its pack.

A group of wolves was an entirely different beast, but not one I couldn't handle.

"Get in the truck," I commanded the women, grabbing two of the wolves by their scruff at vampire speed and bashing their heads together.

The sirens could move faster than the wolves. If they ran, they could get to safety quickly enough to avoid a negative outcome.

The wolves I'd knocked together collapsed, and I grabbed the head of a third, twisting it harshly to the side until his spine snapped.

A set of teeth tore into my shoulder, and I grabbed the muzzle of the wolf they belonged to. Dropping to a knee, I used the momentum to throw him over my shoulder. Before his body had time to collide with the cement, I had sliced through his throat with my fangs.

A pained cry behind me had me roaring, spinning around to find my female on the ground, trapped between three wolves. All three of them were bleeding in various locations,

but there was a gash on my mate's head. Blood was dripping down her nose, mixing with the glitter on her face.

The wolves bumped her, snapping their teeth as they closed
in. There was defiance in Blair's gaze, but dizziness too.

Fury blazed through me in a way I'd never imagined. My
actions became instinct as I lunged.

My fangs tore through another throat.

I snapped another spine.

The third wolf was dead and bleeding before I got to it,
with my mate's knee on his chest, her hands coated in
blood.

I wanted to snap at her for continuing to risk her life in the
fight—but I could hear more wolves coming from inside the
building.

There was no time for an argument.

I grabbed Blair by the waist and ran her to the moving
truck, tossing her in before I slammed the door down and
locked it from the outside.

My chest heaved as I turned to face the incoming wolves.

Usually, my bloodlust would've pushed me through a fight.
But the need to protect my mate seemed to be just as strong
—if not stronger.

I tore through wolf after wolf until I held the throat of the
last one in my hand. A wolf pack had a mental bond that
was unrivaled by anything else. Their alpha would be able

to see and hear anything that happened to them, if he focused on them.

I knew Curtis well enough to be damn sure he was watching the crew he'd sent to my female's home.

"These sirens are *mine*," I snarled. "Every wolf you send for them will face the same fate. If you *ever* make my female bleed again, there's not a wall in the manor that will keep me from finding you and tearing your throat out too."

With that, I ended the wolf's life.

Her body joined her packmates' on the ground, and I stormed back to the moving truck. Getting the lock open and yanking the door up only took a moment, but my female was sitting right inside, looking pissed.

And dizzy.

"What the fuck were you thinking?" I demanded, grabbing her by the waist and hauling her into her family's house at vampire speed. Her sisters followed us. Over my shoulder, I told them, "Pack what you need quickly. Curtis will have others on their way already."

Thankfully, the women could move at vampire speed.

"I know how to fight," Blair said defensively. "I thought there were too many wolves for you to deal with all of them. I—"

I sat her down on the countertop beside the sink in her kitchen, and she clutched the edge of it like her head was spinning.

"What did they do?" I growled.

"Shoved my face into the ground. One of them snapped at the other afterward. I don't think they were supposed to hurt me."

I wet a clean rag and started cleaning as much blood off her face as I could. The shirt she wore—*my* shirt—was wet with it, and it was all over the middle of her face. The glitter seemed to be coming off with the blood, which only made me hate Curtis more.

"I can handle far more than a few wolves, little siren," I said, my anger fading slightly. "There's a reason I lead the vampires. I've spent much of my life training and fighting."

I couldn't blame her for not realizing the extent of my abilities. She had never lived in the Manor, and she interacted with the magical world as little as possible. There would inevitably be things she didn't know.

"If I'd realized, I would've hidden with my sisters," she said. "I was no match for the wolves anyway. It's been too many years since I had to fight anyone, and even then, it was just practice."

"You killed one of them. Curtis didn't send any of his best fighters, but taking down a creature their size is still impressive."

"He wasn't allowed to hurt me," she pointed out.

"Take the victory anyway." I finished cleaning off her face, and pressed the wet rag to her still-bleeding wound. "You might need stitches."

She made a face. "I haven't been to see a doctor in more than a decade."

"Time to break the streak, then." I carried her out to the truck, setting her down in the passenger seat and buckling her in. "I'll pack your things. If you move from this chair, I'll have no choice but to tie you to my side."

"You've threatened that before."

"It's almost like I'm daring you to let me do it," I remarked, pressing her hand harder to her forehead. "Hold the pressure, like this."

She nodded, and I fought the urge to kiss her before I sped back into her house to pack her things.

ten

BLAIR

MY SISTERS all stopped at the moving truck to make sure I was okay, but Damian barked orders at them before we could have a real conversation. On the way out, I'd noticed that our things were strewn around the room, some of them torn, broken, and ruined. I wanted to ask them about it, but he didn't give me time.

"They would've had to track your van to find this place," he said. "You won't be able to drive it again. It stays here. Get in the back of the moving truck. I'll drive carefully."

My sisters exchanged unhappy—and uncertain— expressions.

"We don't have any other choice," I told them quietly, still pressing the damp rag to my forehead as hard as I could. My body was trembling, and I wasn't sure if that was from shock, fear, or blood loss.

The girls nodded, and got in the back of the truck. Damian sped back inside for pillows and blankets, and I noticed multiple tears and bite marks in his clothes. Many of them were bloody.

Worry clenched in my abdomen.

Was he okay?

I hadn't even asked.

Though a magical being could survive losing their mate, the bond would remain permanently. It would make me miss him desperately, too.

I didn't want to experience that. Not even a little.

He closed and locked the back of the truck behind my sisters, and was in the driver's seat a moment later. Leaning over the gap between us, he lifted my hand and my rag, checking my wound.

A growl escaped him, and he pressed it harder to my cut.

"You're bleeding too," I said.

"I'm fine." He grabbed his phone just long enough to send a message, then dropped it and pulled away from my home.

My gaze lingered on the building that had represented safety for so long. It hurt like hell to know we would never be able to go back.

I wasn't going to argue with Damian about his health. We were only mates because he'd given me no other choice.

"Did the wolves go through our things?"

He made a noise of confirmation. "The equipment for your online stores was destroyed. Most of your clothing was covered in wolf urine, or just plain torn to pieces. I'll pay for it all to be replaced."

"We have plenty of money," I whispered, as we turned away from my home. "We can replace it ourselves. Clem and Zora love online shopping. They'll have fun with it."

My phone vibrated in my pocket.

I knew my sisters well enough to know it was someone sending a text to Clementine in our group chat, letting her know that our stuff was destroyed.

It vibrated again, and again, and again.

He jerked his head in a nod. "I can ask Louise to stop at a clothing store in town so you have things to wear until yours arrive."

"My phone keeps going off, so I'm sure she's already ordering things. We had to buy everything online in the first place, so it's not hard to reorder. In a day or two, I'm sure we'll have plenty to wear, so we can save Lou a trip."

He made a noise of frustration, but didn't argue further.

I leaned the side of my head against the window, closing my eyes.

The rest of the drive passed quickly, and soon enough, we were in the vampires' underground parking garage again.

I felt intensely dizzy when Damian opened the passenger door, unbuckling my seat belt and lifting me out like I weighed nothing.

If my world hadn't been spinning, I might've insisted that I could walk.

But it was.

So I didn't.

I realized there was a swarm of vampires around us when Damian gave a few commands without setting me down on my feet.

Open the back of the truck.

Help my sisters out.

Get them anything they need.

It occurred to me just how loud the garage had been when a set of elevator doors closed around us, silencing the noise.

I lifted my arms to wrap around Damian's neck, and the lightest brush of his emotions rolled through me. I couldn't tell what they were exactly, but they felt nice anyway. Nice, but maybe a little too intimate.

I wasn't drinking them in—but I could feel them.

That was the reason I'd agreed to seal the bond in the first place, so I shouldn't have been surprised by it. But, I was.

"You need to feed," he said. "It'll help you heal."

It was tempting.

Very tempting.

Just feeling his emotions the way I was made me hungry.

"You're hurt, though," I murmured.

"Your magic gives me energy. If anything, it'll help me."

That seemed like valid reasoning. So, I let myself take in some of the emotions I could feel.

I was so dizzy that I couldn't tell one from another, but they felt incredible.

Some part of me felt the elevator stop moving and heard it ding, but I didn't move.

Damian didn't either.

His back was against the elevator's wall, his hold on me not tight, but very much possessive.

The elevator dinged again, and I felt more than heard Damian's growl at the owners of the voices I could hear outside it.

The doors closed again, and he hit two buttons.

The elevator stopped.

I finally released his emotions a few minutes later, so insanely sated that I nearly fell asleep. If not for the pain in my forehead, I would've.

My dizziness faded quickly as Damian pressed another

button, and the elevator rose again. Though nothing was spinning anymore, I still felt really out of it.

A few minutes later, we were inside a room that smelled like cleaning supplies.

My eyes closed as Damian set me carefully on a bed. His voice was low as he spoke with someone else, and a polite woman's voice filled my ears soon enough.

"Hi, Blair. I've got a shot here to help with the pain. You'll feel a small pinch on your arm. Your body is trying to heal itself, so you'll probably fall asleep as soon as the pain eases. I'll be handling your stitches while you're unconscious, okay? It'll be numb, so you won't feel anything."

I think I nodded.

I felt a large, strong hand on my arm, and assumed it was Damian's. When I reached for it, he laced his fingers through mine.

The feeling was comforting.

The prick she'd promised arrived, and shortly after, I was lost to sleep.

I WASN'T sure how much time had passed when I finally opened my eyes. I could hear my sisters talking quietly nearby, but the first thing I saw was Damian.

He was still holding my hand, but the gigantic man was sitting in a chair beside my bed, bent awkwardly and using the hospital mattress as a pillow while he slept beside me.

Though he was wearing a clean shirt that didn't have any holes in it, I could see darker spots on the black fabric where he'd clearly bled through it. There was enough blood crusted in his hair to tell me that he hadn't showered, either, though his hands were clean.

Mine were too.

I realized I was wearing a fresh, long-sleeved shirt of Damian's, with my hair tied up out of my face. When I reached up, I felt a messy bun on top of my head that I knew I hadn't made.

My sisters noticed the movement, and came over to greet me. They explained that they'd changed me at the doctor's request, and tied my hair up because there was so much blood in it.

I thanked them, asking the typical questions one would in a hospital and focusing on the information they gave me.

I'd been out for about a day, but my forehead was already mostly healed.

The doctor would be back to remove my stitches soon.

All in all, the situation could've been much worse.

I shooed them out when Izzy's stomach growled, agreeing to text them when I was ready to meet up.

When they were gone, I settled back against my pillow, my gaze moving to Damian once more.

Was he still bleeding?

Had someone given him a blood bag?

He needed to drink blood to recover, didn't he?

I didn't know enough about vampires to say for sure. I'd need to ask around so I could learn how everything worked for them, especially how often they needed to feed. Despite everything, I hadn't forgotten his promise in the throne room to bite me whenever he was hungry.

I was so focused on my thoughts, I didn't notice the woman who walked into the room until she cleared her throat.

I jumped a little, sucking in a breath as she caught me off guard. Damian stirred, but thankfully, stayed asleep.

"Sorry to scare you," she apologized, her voice gentle so as not to wake up Damian. The woman was stunning, with dark skin and curly black hair cut short. Her massive blue eyes were lined with a cat-eye that made them pop, especially given the white coat she had on.

"I'm Kara. I'm technically a medical doctor, but just call me by my name," she said, sitting down in a chair across from Damian's. She grabbed a remote and hit a button to raise the angle of the back half of the bed so I was sitting up. "How are you feeling?"

"Totally normal," I admitted.

"Good. Are you ready to get these stitches out?"

When I confirmed, she grabbed her tools and started working on my forehead carefully.

"Hale said you fed on him after the attack?" she asked, as she worked.

I murmured my confirmation.

"I'm sure that's the reason these healed so quickly. An unmated parasitic being would usually need about three days to handle a wound like this one, even fully-fed. Mate bonds enhance healing, but the amount of the enhancement typically depends on how powerful the bonded beings are. Considering Hale's strength, I shouldn't be surprised by how quickly it worked."

"But you are?"

"I am," she admitted.

"In what ways is he stronger than most vampires?" I asked. No one had ever explained that to me.

"He's faster. Much faster, when he wants to be. Physically stronger, too, hence his ability to take down as many wolves as he did at your home. The real problem with power for vampires comes with its requirement, though."

"What do you mean?"

"The more he relies on his strength, the more blood he burns through. The more blood he burns, the more he needs to drink. And the more he drinks, the more bloodlust he has to fight. He's trained himself not to use his enhanced abilities unless he has no other choice, to preserve his sanity."

"But now that we're mated, he doesn't have to deal with the bloodlust. Right?"

"As long as he drinks your blood."

"That should make it easier, shouldn't it?"

"Assuming he feeds as often as he should."

"You say that like you don't think he does, or will," I countered.

She didn't answer right away, continuing to tug my stitches free. The sensations weren't pleasant, but they didn't hurt.

Finally, she removed the last one and set her tools down on the bed beside me, meeting my gaze.

"Hale is very stubborn," she finally said. "I've known him a long time. Longer than most people in the Manor. His bloodlust was always so strong that he refused to drink from the vein since he was a teenager. He doesn't think he can fight it well enough not to kill his blood sources. Considering his tremendous amount of control, I'm inclined to believe him. Has he bitten you?"

I nodded. "He drinks from me."

"That's good. I would have to imagine he's not taking more than what he deems necessary, though."

I frowned. "So he's too hungry to use his power?"

"Not too hungry to use it, but too hungry to sustain it." She gestured toward him. "He's still bleeding."

My stomach clenched.

I'd been afraid of that.

"It's been an entire day," I said.

She nodded. "He refused to let me look at his injuries until you were healed. I didn't argue. There's usually no point in fighting with him."

"You could've bandaged them when he passed out," I protested.

She gave me a wry smile. "He doesn't have the power to heal them enough to stop bleeding right now, so bandages are useless. I brought in a dozen blood bags, but he didn't bat an eye at them. The only blood he's willing to drink is yours."

The knot in my stomach tightened further. "I need to feed him. I get it. What else are you trying to say, though? I'd appreciate it if you just came out and said it."

Her smile widened a little. "I like you, Blair. I think you're good for him. But the thing you have to understand is that Hale will take care of everyone around him, no matter what it costs him. He'll go to war with the wolves if he has to, even if he doesn't have the blood or energy reserves to manage it. He'll burn himself to the ground protecting you and your sisters if you let him."

I bit my lip.

"You don't have any real reason to want to take care of him right now, but the bond between you is permanent. You need to think long and hard about whether you're willing to spend your immortal life alone if he burns out because you choose not to help him."

I let out a slow breath. "I'll consider it."

She picked up a small syringe with a tiny needle. "This is a medication created to boost blood regeneration. It was designed to help humans and magical beings recover after a vampire lost control of their bloodlust and fed for too long. We realized a few years ago that it has another benefit— boosting blood supply over time. If someone with magic goes through a series of regular injections, it impacts their body long-term, training their magic to regenerate their blood quickly. After the series of injections, it only takes one or two a year to maintain the benefits."

My eyebrows lifted. "Wouldn't that help *everyone*?"

Her smile widened. "Yes, if it was cheap to make. Unfortunately, it's extremely expensive. The other four leaders all went through with the injections and keep up with them."

"Why doesn't Damian?"

"Vampire magic prevents us from regenerating blood at all."

"So it's useless for him. For all of you."

She nodded confirmation. "I highly recommend you go through with the series if you decide you're willing to try to keep up with Damian's appetite. Even if you don't, it's better to be safe than sorry when you're living in a Manor full of vampires. Louise offered to foot the bill already."

I bit my lip.

Lou strode into the room, and I looked at the doorway as she entered. Her gaze went right to her brother, her face settling in a grimace. "He turned down the blood bags again?"

"As expected," Kara agreed.

Lou ran a hand through her hair.

"We're having the talk," Kara said, and Lou's grimace deepened.

"How often does he actually need to feed on me?" I asked.

"Most vampires only need blood once or twice a week, but I analyzed his to look at the rate of cellular turnover," Kara said. "He needs blood every day."

My eyebrows lifted.

"I asked her to," Lou said, sitting down on the arm of Kara's chair. "The first time Hale used his power and nearly burned himself out."

"It's happened before?" My voice raised. "How often?"

"A few times a year," Lou said.

I shoved a hand through my hair.

"He refuses to believe he needs to feed more than twice a week, and he always drinks from blood bags," she added.

"Why do the blood bags matter?"

"They contain a set amount of blood. When you drink from the vein, your fangs retract when you've had enough. You keep drinking when you're lost to bloodlust, but your fangs aren't in the picture," Lou explained.

I racked my brain, trying to remember if I'd ever felt his teeth naturally retract while in my skin. I couldn't remember that happening, but I was usually relaxed and horny when he drank from me. So, I didn't think I'd remember even if it had happened.

"He wouldn't be in this bad of shape if he drank enough from you before the fight," Kara clarified.

"So he was hungry even before the wolves?"

"He's hungry *constantly*," Lou said.

I leaned back against my bed. "The injections just make my body create more blood? Do they change it in any way? Will it taste different, or force him to drink more, or become more addictive or anything?"

Both women shook their heads.

"The man is bent over your hospital bed, slowly bleeding out, Blair. He doesn't need any help becoming addicted to you," Kara said.

She wasn't wrong.

"They're not addictive for *me*, right? And they wouldn't hurt me if I stopped them?"

"No. There are no side effects."

"I'm not going to commit to trying to convince him to feed from me every day," I said, "But I'll think about it, and try to pay more attention to his hunger. For now, I'll try the first injection so I can get him to drink more from me today. I'd like to see copies of whatever medical studies have been done with it before I think about getting the rest."

"See, I knew I liked you," Kara said easily. "So much common sense."

Lou looked relieved. "Thank you."

I nodded.

The injection was mostly painless, and over quickly. I didn't feel any different at all afterward, which seemed like a good sign.

They asked me a few questions about the attack before Kara told me I was set to leave whenever I was ready. She promised to lock the door on the way out so I had privacy with Hale.

Then, the two of them left.

I'd been itching to get my hands in Damian's hair again since I'd woken up, so I let myself bury my fingers in. It was a little crusty with blood, and there was still glitter in it, but he had saved me and my sisters so I didn't care about that.

He didn't stir as I touched his hair, or rubbed his scalp lightly.

I debated putting my arm beneath his mouth and just trying to wedge his teeth against it to feed him, but that didn't seem like a great idea. As soon as he recovered enough to realize what was going on, he would release my arm.

If I was going to get him to lose control long enough to feed heavily from me, I needed to be more strategic.

The last few times he'd bitten me, he'd put himself in the power position. He had been on top of me, pinning me, or holding me firmly. He'd been in control.

But in the nightclub, he'd bitten me by accident.

The man didn't drink from *anyone*, yet I'd made him forget himself enough to bite me.

Honestly, I was kind of proud of that.

So, I knew what I needed to do.

I pushed his shoulders, trying to get him off the bed. At first, he didn't move, so I pushed harder.

"Damian," I said loudly, trying to wake him up a little.

He stirred a little.

I repeated his name two more times, pushing more.

He slowly peeled himself off the mattress.

His expression told me he was barely conscious, but thankfully, he leaned back in his chair.

"Stitches out?" he mumbled.

"Yeah, I'm totally fine," I said, slipping off the mattress and sitting down on his lap. His hands didn't even go to my waist, which told me exactly how out of it he was.

Rather than trying to prod him or seduce him, I kissed him, tugging lightly at his emotions. My magic would wake him up a little more, energizing him. I wouldn't take much from him while he was so weak, but a little push of my power would do wonders.

When his fingers landed on my hips, I released him and met his heavy gaze. "Bite me, Damian."

His chest rumbled violently, and his teeth were in my throat before my heart had time to beat again.

His magic felt weak against my skin, barely brushing over me at all. He drank from me hungrily, greedily, with sounds of pleasure and satisfaction.

Over a few minutes, his power grew stronger, relaxing me and making me want him.

I felt it when he realized how long he'd been drinking from me and started to slow down. His fangs were still firmly lodged in my throat, so he definitely wasn't full.

I needed to distract him before he started to worry he was taking too much.

Biting my lip, I wrapped my hand around the back of his neck and pulled him against me harder as I yanked on his emotions.

Burning desire.

Fiery lust.

Suppressed hunger.

He growled against my throat, sucking hard, and a heavier wave of his magic hit me.

Something about the intensity of his emotions running through me while his teeth were buried in my throat was absolutely intoxicating.

I rocked my hips, grinding against him as he drank. His cock was hard as stone, his magic making the feel of him even better.

He slowed again, and I took more from him, refusing to let him go.

Intense fear.

Desperate need.

Endless starvation.

I stole the negative emotions, pumping him with the power racing through my veins.

And like a dam breaking, I felt his control snap.

He snarled against my throat, digging his fangs in fully.

I moaned at the wave of need that accompanied it, feeling his demanding grip moving across my bare thighs, over my ass, sliding between my legs. His fingers moved through my slickness, and my desperation reached new heights.

"I need you," I breathed.

My sisters and I all had implants that prevented us from getting pregnant, just to be safe, so that wasn't a concern. And magical beings couldn't get diseases, so condoms were unnecessary.

Unlike the last time, Damian didn't have the control to refuse me.

He released me long enough to free his cock, and I felt the head of him against my opening for the briefest moment before he yanked me down over him.

I let out a choked gasp as every massive inch of him filled me, stretching me and hitting every nerve ending I possessed.

I'd had sex before, but this was something else.

Something bigger.

Something *so much better*.

I lost hold of my magic as he moved my hips, helping me ride him harder and faster than I could've on my own.

He was still drinking from me, his magic hot and heavy even as it made me feel like I'd finally found the place I belonged.

My first climax built up quickly, and I cried out as I lost control around him.

He made a noise of animalistic satisfaction against me, not releasing my hips or slowing my motions. The man wanted more—demanded more—and I wouldn't have turned him down if I could.

I was the one who started this.

I was the one who set him off.

And I would enjoy every minute of the ride.

Damian dragged me to the edge of another orgasm quickly, and my gasps of pleasure earned me another sound of satisfaction from the man.

His fangs began retracting from my skin slowly as I approached my third climax, and he fucked me harder and faster.

When I lost control with a scream, he roared against my throat, flooding my channel with his release.

His fangs finally disappeared as we caught our breath together, the electric magic between us fading slowly as we came down from the high.

"I shouldn't have done that," Damian said, his voice low as he spoke against my ear. His forehead was pressed to my shoulder, so I couldn't see his face.

"That's exactly what a girl wants to hear after the best sex of her life," I panted, my eyes closed. He was still buried inside me, but I could feel our combined release starting to slide slowly down the insides of my thighs.

It wasn't a pleasant feeling—but damn, it was an erotic one.

His grip on my bare ass tightened. "That's not..." He let out a harsh breath. "Not the sex. That was great. But I drank way too much from you. How are you still conscious? How are you feeling?"

"Your doctor injected me with some kind of blood thing," I said. "I'm a little lightheaded, now that we're not screwing anymore, but I'm fine otherwise."

"If you had an injection, there's no fucking reason for you to be lightheaded," he bit out. "I took too much."

"You weren't healing. You needed the blood. I'm fine," I insisted.

"Kara shouldn't have left you alone with me when she knew I was this hungry." He stood up, and I bit back a moan at the way his cock drove deeper inside me with the motion.

Then, he set me on the edge of the bed and pulled out.

I wanted to hook my ankles around his ass and tell him not to leave, but something told me I'd already pushed him too much.

And now that I wasn't on his lap, the world *was* kind of spinning.

Despite the spinning, I could see his face enough to realize that I'd done the right thing.

His skin had a lot more color than I'd ever seen. His face looked stronger. His entire body looked thicker. Hell, even those gorgeous, piercing blue eyes looked brighter.

The man had been starving himself, and I hadn't even realized.

"I'm fine," I insisted.

"Lay down. It's going to take a few hours for your blood to regenerate," he growled. "I have a doctor to kill."

With that, he sped out of the room so fast, I couldn't even tell him not to hurt her.

Sighing, I stared up at the ceiling.

Though Damian was a violent bastard, and insanely strong, I knew he wouldn't kill his old friend. So, I didn't bother going after him.

As soon as I was steady enough, I would sink to the bottom of the pool and let the water make all of my problems disappear for a while.

eleven

BLAIR

WHEN I GOT out of bed, I realized that I had a new problem.

Damian had locked the door from the outside.

Anger blazed through me.

I went to all the effort of feeding his grumpy, starving ass, and he locked me in a hospital room?

There wasn't even a shower! Just a toilet in the corner!

What was wrong with him?

Luckily, my phone was on the table beside the bed.

I made my way over to it slowly, pausing for a moment to grab the back of a chair when I nearly collapsed. After I was steady again, I finally got the phone and sat back down on the edge of the bed.

Considering the many intricacies of the situation, I couldn't risk calling Zora or Izzy. They would hate Damian if they learned that he'd locked me in, and they'd refuse to acknowledge my own fault in the situation. Both of them could hold grudges like no one else.

Clementine and Zora were the closest of all of us, so I couldn't call Clem. Zora would find out, and that grudge would happen anyway.

But I did have one sister who I could trust to keep a secret, without holding it against Damian. Considering I was going to spend my entire immortal life with him, that seemed somewhat important.

I dialed her number and lifted my phone to my ear. She answered immediately.

"Hello?"

"Hey, Avery." My voice sounded a little weaker than it should've. Whoops.

Maybe I shouldn't have pushed Damian *quite* so hard.

"I did something stupid but necessary," I said. "Damian locked me in the hospital room because of it, but I really need to go for a swim. Can you swing a rescue without getting any of the other girls involved?"

"Mmhm. Give me a second."

I heard her call out to one of the other girls that she was going to her room. A minute later, I heard an elevator ding.

"Okay, I'm on my way. I don't think I want the full story, but I probably need it if I'm going to avoid losing my head when your vampire comes looking."

"Kara, the doctor, told me he's been starving himself because he's afraid of losing control of his bloodlust. She gave me this injection to help me recover after he drinks from me. I sort of pushed him into drinking until he was completely sated, while we screwed. He said he was going to kill her afterward, told me to stay in here while I recover, and ran off." I ran a hand over the top of my blood-crusted hair.

"So he's coming back for you soon," she said.

"I don't know. Maybe."

"If he's worried enough about you that he locked you in a hospital room, it seems safe to say he is."

"Maybe. But I don't want to be here when he does. He's going to be pissed."

Avery laughed softly. "I'm not swimming with you. I'm going to hide in my room like a coward after your jailbreak. When he's not on the warpath anymore, text me so I know I can come out."

The doorknob twisted, and she stepped into the room, lowering her phone from her ear.

I surged to my feet, nearly crashing to the ground when my knees knocked together.

Though I caught myself on the chair, she rushed over to catch me too. There was concern in her eyes.

"How much did he drink from you?"

"Probably enough to kill me without that injection," I said cheerfully, easing myself away from the chair and pulling her toward the door.

"Blair!" Her eyes were wide with worry. "You *can't* do that."

"It was a one-time thing," I insisted. "If I can get him to start drinking from me every day, he won't be starving anymore, and he won't need to take nearly that much blood. When my magic and the medicine work, I'll be perfectly fine. I just have to go through with a series of injections—it's not a big deal."

As the words left me, I couldn't believe I was saying them.

I hadn't even agreed to go through with it yet.

I hadn't even told Kara I'd let her inject me again.

But some part of me knew that I would anyway, scientific studies I hadn't read yet be damned.

"That's literally insane," Avery protested, as we walked to the elevator together.

"We're mated permanently. What's the alternative?"

"Let him starve?"

I scowled at her. "Starving is miserable. I did it too, remember? I couldn't stand kissing strangers. It's only been two days—or three, maybe—since I started drinking from him, but the way I feel is so much different. I'm not letting him starve just because he's afraid of hurting me."

"If the fear is an actual possibility, it's reasonable," she argued.

"I'm his blood mate. It has to work," I insisted. "Especially with the injections."

"I can't keep this a secret for you. If you're risking your life, our sisters need to know."

"I'll tell them myself, after I swim and recover."

"And deal with your vampire on a warpath," she pointed out.

"That too."

"You can't put it off," she warned.

"I won't. I'll explain it. I just have to talk to Damian first."

Or Kara, at the very least.

Maybe Lou, too.

They would be in on my plan even if my sisters were against it.

And as much as I couldn't believe that was my plan, I had *seen* the way he physically changed. He needed blood. *My* blood. It would make him stronger, which meant he could protect my sisters and everyone else in the Manor that much better.

That was the only reason I cared.

...wasn't it?

I pushed the uncertainty aside and squeezed Avery's arm as we reached the pool.

"*Please* reconsider this plan," she said.

"I can't, but thank you for rescuing me. I love you."

"I love you too," she said grudgingly, leaving me beside the most beautiful pool in the world as she headed back to the elevator.

Sitting down on one of the massive rocks at the side of the pool, I slipped my feet in the water and made a group chat with two of the phone numbers I found programmed into the device.

ME
Operation Feed Starving Vampire is a go

LOU
I know, I just got snarled at by a furious, extremely healthy looking vamp. He's looking for you, Kare

KARA
I'm hiding in a friend's room. He'll calm down long before he finds me. How good does he look?

ME
Fucking gorgeous

LOU
As much as it pains me to admit, even I can't disagree

KARA

Take a picture for the rest of us next time

LOU

According to Hale, she was too busy nearly keeling over

We may have gone a little too far

KARA

The mate bond's magic won't let him kill her. When his fangs are buried in her, they're connected enough that he can sense her life force, even if he's not conscious of it yet

ME

Well that makes me feel better

You should've started with that

KARA

I thought everyone knew

LOU

Not everyone took Medicine for Magical Beings, Kare

KARA

Apparently not

OOOH HE DOES LOOK HOT

LOU

Ohhh shit

My forehead creased.

ME

What happened?

I missed something

Kara sent me a screenshot of the Vamp Manor Homies group chat. There was a picture of a furious-looking Damian storming through the dining hall with a monstrous plate of food, his light skin golden with life and his hair still crusted with blood.

The message beneath it said,

JEN

Big Daddy Hale's on a rampage. Looks like he had a little extra siren soup for lunch. Big Mama B totally took a dick for the team!

I snorted so hard, I swear I nearly choked.

ME

Please tell me I'm not Big Mama B

KARA

Girl, don't lie to yourself

He's about to force-feed you until you're bloated so he can yell at you

ME

Think he can hold his breath long enough to dive to the bottom of his new pool?

KARA

*YOUR new pool

LOU

I'm not sure

ME

Guess we'll find out

Wish me luck

> And get the rest of the injections ready, I'm gonna need them

I hit the button to turn off my phone, peeled his shirt over my head, and dove in bare-assed.

If he was going to lock me in a hospital room after fucking my brains out, he was going to learn the hard way that I wouldn't take his bullshit lying down.

Big Mama B was no pushover.

...and I was never calling myself that again.

Vamp Manor was totally screwing with my head.

twelve

BLAIR

THE WATER immediately soothed my tense muscles and eased the adrenaline racing through my veins.

I took my time swimming to the bottom of the pool, and when I got there, let out a slow breath as I settled along the smooth basin of it on my front. Propping my cheek on my arm, I closed my eyes and enjoyed the silence.

There was just something peaceful about water that nothing else could ever compare to. It was blissful.

Tranquil.

Calmin—

A pair of thick arms banded around my middle, and I shrieked into the water as I was yanked upward and dragged toward the surface. My back was to a chiseled bare chest, and as soon as the initial shock faded, I knew exactly who the arms belonged to.

We broke through the water a minute later, and Damian hauled me onto a rock, glaring at me while his gorgeous chest heaved. "I locked you in that room."

"I had no problem opening the door," I said innocently, my chest rising and falling quickly as I recovered from the surprise. "And I didn't think you could hold your breath that long. I knew vampires could last a while beneath the water, but damn."

"I wouldn't build my mate a pool I couldn't swim to the bottom of," he growled back. "And that's not what we're talking about. You let me nearly drain you dry, and you were fucking *gone* when I got back with food."

Whispers around the corner met my ears.

"If a picture of my mate naked is uploaded or sent anywhere, all parties involved will be removed from Mistwood and inserted into a tiny clan in the middle of nowhere," Damian said loudly, his voice ringing with authority.

The whispers cut off abruptly.

One last voice said, "Sorry," and I heard the footsteps grow quieter as the intruders walked away.

Finally, we were alone again.

"What did I say about your swimwear?" he asked, shoving a hand through his damp, crusty, tangled hair.

Yeah, I felt a little bad about that.

Not the lack of swimwear—the hair.

I lifted a hand to mine, and winced when I remembered that I hadn't washed it. Thankfully, my magic would cut through and purify any gunk in the water. Including my blood.

"I told you I wasn't arguing about that anymore," I said.

"You're going to make me lose my fucking mind," he snarled, shoving a hand through his hair again. "You need to eat. You couldn't even focus your eyes on me when I was done feeding you. I'm going back to the fucking blood bags. I—" I grabbed him by the hair, since his shirt was discarded next to mine.

And, because I didn't know what else to do, I kissed him.

Hard.

When I slipped my tongue into his mouth and took some of his fury and fear away, he let out a long breath and kissed me back.

Just for a moment, though.

When he pulled away, he still looked pretty pissed. "We're not done talking about this."

"We're *not* talking about it. You're lecturing me."

"I'm not lecturing you."

I lifted an eyebrow.

He scowled. "If you'd start listening to me, I wouldn't have to lecture you."

"Oh please, the last thing you need is a submissive mate. You'd walk all over the poor, delicate thing."

He flashed me his fangs. "At least she wouldn't let me drain her dry."

"Our bond won't let you kill me."

"*Theoretically.*"

I rolled my eyes. "Has any vampire ever killed their blood mate before?"

I didn't know much about Kara, but I had the feeling that she wouldn't spout information that wasn't factual, or at least pretty damn near that.

"No," he admitted. "But there's never been a vampire as powerful as I am with a blood mate."

"It has nothing to do with power, though. Kara said that our bond connects you to my life force while you're drinking from me, so you can tell if you ever take too much. Which you didn't."

"Of course Kara put you up to this. Lou was involved too, wasn't she?"

Oops.

I was supposed to be calming him down so he *didn't* want to kill them.

"I'm starving," I said, reaching for the food tray he'd set next to the edge of the pool. It was close enough to the rock that I could reach it if I stretched. "And you look amazing with this much blood in your system."

Both facts were true.

He grabbed my wrist. "You're eating in our room, where I know no one is going to walk up and see those perfect little tits."

Right, I was naked.

And even more glittery than I'd been before my swim.

Glitter aside, he'd never seen me naked before.

I probably should've cared that this was the first time, but considering he'd had both his hand and cock inside me, a little nudity didn't really seem like a big deal.

And I'd seen *him* naked, so it was kind of necessary to level the playing field.

Not that I wanted it *level*.

I wanted to be in complete control until he agreed to my terms. He had his turn being in charge when he made me agree to a mate bond in exchange for my sisters' safety.

Maybe it would give him the *feeling* of us being level, at least. That would give me even more control.

"I think that was an insult," I said, reaching for my shirt instead.

If he wanted to eat in our room, that was fine. I'd let him control that.

"I called your tits perfect. How is that an insult?"

"You called them little. Societal expectations require breasts to be big to be attractive."

He scowled.

Then he grabbed me off the rock, set me on his lap, and took one of those *perfect little tits* in his mouth, sucking hard enough to make me swear.

And squirm.

He cupped the other one in his hand, stroking my nipple with his thumb while he dragged his tongue around the first.

He licked.

Sucked.

Nipped with his teeth.

And by the time he released me, I was panting and wet for him yet again.

"Convinced I like them yet?" he drawled, when he finally set my bare ass back down on the rock.

"You are a *terrible* tease." I caught my breath as he grabbed my shirt.

Well, *his* shirt.

I held my hand out for it, but instead of giving it to me, he pulled it over his own head. "Since you're so obsessed with being naked in public, you obviously don't need any clothes to wear on your way to the elevator."

My eyes narrowed as he stood smoothly. "You are *not* going to convince me to have that argument."

"I didn't say I was." He picked up my food, and gestured for me to walk in front of him.

Biting back a harsh reply that would only make him feel like he'd won, I put a smile on my face as I grabbed my phone and stood, striding in front of him so my bare ass was directly in his view. "Well, I'm *so* glad you've decided you're comfortable with me being naked all the time. It'll be a relief not to wear your oversized shirts and sweatpants anymore."

"I'm sure." His murmur was one of appreciation, and my lips threatened to curve in a smile.

"I'm feeling like taking the stairs, Big Daddy Hale," I called over my shoulder as we reached a hallway intersection. I could still feel his release dripping down my thighs, so I obviously hadn't swam for long enough. Maybe I should've scrubbed down there or something. "Left or right?"

He muttered something that sounded like, "Fuck me."

"I already did, and you forgot to even acknowledge it," I tossed back, deciding to go with left.

He followed me without pause, which made me think I'd picked the right way. "I acknowledged it."

"*It was great* isn't a compliment when a woman tells you it was the best sex of her life. You basically said *I've had better.* You could at least mention what I did wrong." As the words came out, I was forced to admit to myself that he'd hurt me just the tiniest bit.

Well, fine.

Maybe more than the tiniest bit.

I'd only had sex a few times, so it wasn't like I was a professional. And I'd never left afterward saying, *"I want to do that again."*

So yeah, maybe I was shit in bed.

But I didn't want to *hear* that.

Maybe I needed to ask my sisters for pointers or something. I—

He grabbed my hip, turning me around and walking me backward until my ass met a cold wall. I tried not to shiver.

His eyes were narrowed at me when I looked up. "I haven't had better. Between sating myself on your blood, fucking you while I fed, and feeling you come around me three times, that was the most erotic experience of my life. I just shouldn't have let it happen."

"And there you go again." I tossed a hand toward him, hurt and anger still curled in my abdomen.

"Powerful vampires should never have sex while they feed, Blair. It's addictive. People get hurt. I should never have risked your life the way I did, and I am *never* going to be okay with what happened, regardless of how fucking good it felt."

"Do most vampires refrain from screwing their blood mates?"

His scowl answered my question.

I pushed his hands off me, and started back down the hall-way. A door opened behind us, and he snarled at the person to wait five minutes.

The door shut again quickly.

My phone vibrated in my hand, and I looked down at the screen.

The message said I had been invited to join VAMP MANOR HOMIES.

Biting back a grin, I hit accept.

My phone vibrated repeatedly, until I muted the chat and pulled it up to see the messages.

"Who are you texting?" Damian still sounded frustrated.

"No one."

A message popped up.

> **SYLVESTER**
> Hale just snarled at me. Think I saw Blair's bare ass in front of him
>
> **ALLIE**
> Big Mama B isn't taking it lying down

Damn straight I wasn't.

Damian plucked my phone from my hand, ignoring my noise of irritation as he read the messages.

"You don't want to be a part of that chat," he grumbled, handing it back.

"Whatever you say, Big Daddy Hale."

He swatted my ass, making me laugh in protest and take a few steps forward. My legs were still a little shaky, so I tripped a tiny bit as I did. He caught me with a growl and an arm around my waist.

"See why this is a bad idea?"

"If you hadn't been starving yourself before, you wouldn't have needed so much blood, and I would be perfectly fine," I said.

"Stop listening to Lou."

"I'm pretty sure talking to your sister is a normal part of being your mate."

He grunted. "I wasn't starving."

"The way your skin is basically glowing right now proves that wrong. Kara says you should be feeding every day."

"Kara is full of shit."

"And scientific knowledge."

"No one needs to feed every day."

"Normal rules don't apply to you, and you know it."

We finally reached the staircase. Instead of letting me walk up it in front of him like I'd been planning, he scooped me up and threw me over his shoulder, holding my thighs so I didn't tumble off.

He took the stairs two at a time, and wasn't breathing hard when he reached our living space, a few stories up.

After tossing me onto the bed, he put the tray of food down next to me. "Eat, Blair. I'm not joking. If you leave this room without emptying that tray, I will assign you an around-the-clock guard. No more swimming naked. No more walking around hungry, with your magic drawing people to you. No more—"

"I agreed to be your mate, not your prisoner," I snapped.

"My *mate* should know better than to force me to drink more than I need, risking her life in the process. I'm done fucking around."

"You are *such* an asshole."

"In the flesh." He gestured to himself sarcastically. "I have work to do."

"Fine, starve yourself," I called behind him, as he walked out. "Two can play that game, too."

The door shut behind him, and I huffed as I grabbed the first plate of food with one hand, sending a text to Lou and Kara.

ME

He's pissed about the feeding thing.
Knows you two are involved. I'm sorry

KARA

He's been pissed at us for bringing it up for
ages. Don't feel bad on our behalf

LOU

What happened?

ME

Long story, but basically, he threatened to assign me a guard if I keep pushing him. Convo ended when he stormed out. I may have threatened to starve myself if he refuses to eat enough

KARA

Fuckkkkk

I am not getting behind that plan

LOU

You starving yourself isn't the answer here

ME

I'm not feeding on him if he's not feeding on me

LOU

Just give him space for a few days and he'll come around.

KARA

Don't starve yourself, though

ME

Fine.

It was a lie.

Despite Lou's words, I *didn't* think he'd come around.

We were evenly matched, as far as stubbornness went. The only reason I'd been able to force myself to feed every month was because the alternative was dying and leaving my sisters alone. I truly, whole-heartedly despised kissing strangers and drinking from them that much.

The vampire king had finally met his match, because I would *not* let him win. I'd play along with his rules for a few days, but if he wasn't feeding, he could watch his mate go hungry alongside him.

And even though I was aware that was a horrible, absolutely toxic way to make my point, I was also sure it was the best option.

So, I was all in.

thirteen

DAMIAN

BLAIR WAS UNCHARACTERISTICALLY calm over the next few days.

She wore a one-piece swimsuit one of her sisters had ordered, and her own new clothing.

She was in bed and asleep before me every night, and left before I woke up.

I kept setting my alarm earlier in an attempt to catch her, but it hadn't worked yet.

She answered my texts about her location without snark or sass.

She didn't try to force me to feed on her, or try to seduce me.

By the time a week had passed, I was officially suspicious.

"How often do sirens need to feed?" I asked Clementine,

during dinner. Though I was at their table, and Blair sat beside me, we hadn't touched all week.

Keeping my hands off her was torture. Her glitter was coming off more every day now that her pool was free of chlorine, and it irritated me that I didn't have it on my skin. It was on our sheets—but only on her side of the bed.

And my fucking fangs kept descending for no reason. Now that I'd been fully sated for the first time since I was a teenager, going a week without feeding felt like my stomach was trying to climb its way out of my throat. I usually only drank two blood bags twice a week. I just had to suffer through the initial pain to readjust to that.

Clem looked surprised by the question, but she was the friendliest of the bunch, so I knew she'd answer. "Usually like once a week to stay strong. We feel our best if we feed twice a week, though."

I looked at her sisters, and a few of them nodded in agreement.

I'd thought I felt lust coming off Blair for a few days, but wasn't sure if it was just because of how badly I wanted her. No one had reported feeling affected by it.

Maybe because she was keeping to herself...

I met her gaze, where she was sitting next to me. "You're hungry."

"Am I?"

I narrowed my eyes at her.

She lifted an eyebrow at me. "I'm not eating if you're not."

I growled at her, and she yawned. "Wow, I'm getting tired. About ready to call it a night."

"It's seven PM."

"Late," she agreed.

"Bullshit."

"Okay," she said sweetly, standing up and tucking a long, loose strand of soft, golden hair behind her ear.

My gaze tracked the motion predatorily, and by the time I snapped myself out of it, she was striding across the room.

I stood abruptly, but one of her sisters hooked a foot in the leg of my chair and yanked it back. It caught me off guard, and I sat down.

"We need to talk, asshole," Zora said flatly.

I looked over my shoulder, trying to catch another glimpse of my female, but she was gone.

"The situation between you two is fucked up," Zora said, and I finally looked at her. "Fix it."

"What do you mean, fix it?" I asked.

"She's going to starve herself as long as you refuse to drink enough of her blood. She's been going through with the injections. They make her hungry, and she's fighting it hard," Clementine explained. "You don't want to try to out-stubborn Blair, believe me. If you think her walking down a hallway naked is bad, you have no idea what you're in for."

My nostrils flared at the reminder. "Drinking from her is a risk to her life."

"You'd been bleeding for an entire day the last time you tried it, and you didn't kill her then," Izzy said drily. "How much more could you take from her?"

My jaw set. "I'll negotiate with her. Feeding twice a week would be enough to keep me functioning."

Functioning better than I was at the moment, at least.

"You can try, but Blair doesn't negotiate if she knows she's right," Clementine said with a shrug.

"She's *not* right."

"Your doctor disagrees. It's hard to argue with the scientific data," Izzy said.

My nostrils flared. "I'm trying to protect her. And the rest of you, for that matter."

"Getting our sister's mate killed is a shitty way to protect any of us. Especially her," Zora said. "We were against her plan at first too, but when you talk to your doctor, it becomes pretty obvious that she's right. Pull your head out of your ass and fix it."

I scowled but stood again. "I'll talk to her."

"That didn't sound like an agreement," Clem remarked.

"It wasn't one."

I strode out of the cafeteria, determined to find my mate. She wasn't going hungry on my watch any longer.

. . .

BLAIR WAS CURLED up in our bed with the canopy lowered over her when I got to the bedroom. I raised it, and she shot me an annoyed look. Her hair was wet, and irritation flooded me when I realized I'd missed catching her in the shower.

Again.

My cock fucking hurt with the distance between us.

"Hey," I said, trying to resist the urge to lecture her about starving. Her gaze was wary as I sat down on the edge of the bed. "We need to talk."

She closed her eyes. "I'm not feeding on you. There's nothing to talk about."

"Are you feeding on someone else?" my voice lowered, taking on an edge of something feral.

If one of my vampires was feeding my mate, they wouldn't survive the hour.

"No. I can't, remember? Are you?"

My lips twisted in disgust. "No. The only person I want on my mouth is you."

"On that we agree, if nothing else." Her eyes were still closed.

I dragged a hand through my hair.

She didn't want to talk, and she wasn't going to like my ideas, but I'd offer her everything I could.

"I can't let you starve," I said.

"You can't force me to eat any more than I can force you," she murmured.

"You don't risk my life when you take from me."

"Neither do you."

I made a noise of frustration. "Kara's theory is bullshit."

"It's not a theory if you have factual evidence."

"I don't need to feed every day," I growled back. "Twice a week is enough. I can agree to drink from you twice a week, in exchange for feeding you."

"Okay."

I blinked. "Okay?"

"Sure. Feeding from you once a month is enough to keep me alive, so I'll feed you twice a week, and you can feed me once a month."

My lips twisted in a snarl. "That's not going to happen."

"Then we'll stay at an impasse. That's fine with me. I love a good impasse," she murmured into her pillow.

I shoved another hand through my hair.

My phone rang in my pocket, and I yanked it out. Talon's name was on the screen, so I knew I couldn't get out of answering. "What do you want?"

"Kai finally pulled his ass out of the fae realm. Meeting's on for tonight. Midnight in neutral territory. Bring your siren." He hung up without waiting for confirmation.

Blair must've heard his side of the conversation, because she was already sitting up. "A meeting with who?"

"The rest of the leaders. I tried to set it up right after Curtis's attack, but Kai's been in the fae realm, dealing with his people's shit."

"Have you ever been?" she asked, her curiosity piqued.

"No, and you won't either. No one makes it back from the fae realm without fae magic or a fae mate."

"Damn." Her excitement faded.

"We're not staying at this impasse. This isn't healthy," I growled. "You need to eat. I can't walk you into a room full of the other leaders and have you set off their magic. The last thing I need is Curtis trying to touch you. I'd have no choice but to kill him, and I'd start a war in the process."

"Technically, he wants Clem."

"He can't have any of you."

"Well I'm not feeding on you, so I'll just have to stay here."

"That's not going to work this time. The whole meeting is about you. If I show up with a fresh mate mark without you at my side, they're going to be suspicious."

"Alright. If you want to feed me, you're going to have to drink until you're sated again," she said, matter-of-factly.

My eyes narrowed, but I bit back the response at the tip of my tongue. She had proven that she wasn't going to back down. I'd have to think of another way to make that happen.

Though I didn't respond right away, there was something in her gaze that almost looked... hurt.

"What's wrong?" I asked.

She stood up. "Just go drink from your blood bags. I'll hold your hand while I feed from Lou. She's mated, so you'll know there's nothing sexual about it."

I stepped in front of her before she could walk around the bed. "Absolutely not. I'm not touching the blood bags, and you're not kissing my fucking sister."

"I'd rather kiss her than you right now," Blair tossed back.

A bolt of possessiveness raced down my spine, and I grabbed her hips, walking her backward slowly, toward the nearest wall. Her ass met the surface.

That possessiveness surged with the light pressure of her body against mine, pinned right where I wanted her. "I've been giving you too much space."

"There's no such thing."

"Like hell there isn't." I wrapped my hand around the back of her neck, dragging my thumb over the mark on her throat.

My mark.

"My balls have been blue for days. I keep waking up earlier than you, trying to catch you."

"You won't."

"I'm starting to realize that." I tipped her head just a little to the side, and she let me. Lowering my nose to her throat, I inhaled deeply. "Fuck, you smell good."

"You're not even willing to listen to Kara's research," she said, her voice growing a little tighter and her body stiffening a bit.

That wouldn't do.

Tapping into my magic lightly, I slipped my hand beneath the oversized t-shirt she wore to bed. My knuckles slid over the lace hem of her panties before I caught her hip.

She sucked in a breath when I used my grip to open her thighs a little more, but she did relax slightly.

"Kara's research doesn't matter compared to my gut, and my gut says I don't need to feed that often."

"Have you ever tried?"

"No." I stroked her hipbone lightly with my thumb.

"Alright, you want to make a deal?" she asked.

"Depends on what you're offering."

Her nostrils flared. "If you agree to try drinking from me until you're sated five days a week, I'll let you feed me once a week."

"No." I lowered my mouth to her neck, dragging my tongue over my mark there lightly.

"If you're not going to give me a counteroffer, you can go to your meeting alone and deal with their suspicion."

"I'll feed three times a week, if you feed once."

"No. If you feed three times, you get to feed me every third week."

My nostrils flared. "Little siren..."

"*No*, Damian."

The way she said my name made me want to agree with her just to erase her anger.

"Every other day, then," I said. "For one feeding a week. That's fair.

"That's only three times some weeks," she pointed out.

I sucked lightly on her throat, earning a sharp breath in. "I've felt your magic luring me for days, woman. Once a week isn't enough for you. You need at least two. Probably three. Every other day for me and one feeding for you is fair, even according to Kara's ridiculous standards. Especially if you're forcing me to drink until I'm sated. I'm a fucking endless pit."

"It's the injections that are making me so hungry. I think I have extra blood right now or something."

"You can't have *extra blood*."

"Feels like I can."

I dragged my tongue over her throat, ignoring the way my fangs throbbed and my head started to ache.

I needed her.

But I couldn't bite her until we had an agreement.

"Monday, Wednesday, Friday, and Saturday," she countered. "In exchange for feeding me once a week. If you want two, you have to bite me on Tuesdays too."

"Stubborn little thing," I grumbled, dragging the tips of my fangs over her neck just so I could feel her shiver against me. "Am I allowed to fuck you when I bite you?"

"Depends how good you make it for me."

I growled, dragging my thumb over that sensitive line on her throat again. "I hope that's a challenge."

"It is."

"Monday, Wednesday, Friday, and Saturday it is. I won't agree to more until I see how that affects you. And if I can prove that I don't need more, you have to drop it."

"Deal," she agreed.

I kneeled in front of her, one hand still on her hip as I leaned in close to her core. The scent of her arousal was so strong, it felt like a fist around my cock.

Having my nose right there was enough to drive a man mad with need.

"I thought you were going to bite m—ohhh." She groaned when I dragged my tongue over her clit, through her panties. Her fingers dug into my hair, and my cock fought against the zipper on my jeans.

But I wanted Blair as desperate for me as I was for her, *constantly*.

I wanted her screaming my name in my office while I fucked her during lunch.

Sitting on my face in the middle of the night because she needed my mouth when she woke up from a wet dream.

Walking into our meeting that night with my release dripping down her thighs so every bastard in the room could smell exactly who my little siren belonged to.

My balls clenched with that image.

Fuck, yes.

I wasn't accepting anything less.

fourteen

BLAIR

MY KNEES SHOOK SLIGHTLY as Damian opened them wider.

"You seem uncertain, little siren," he all but purred. Though he was on his knees in front of me, I was under no impression that he was at my mercy. The man was going to take what he wanted—and he was going to enjoy it, if the look in his eyes told me anything.

While I didn't want to give him any of my power, he had just agreed to feed on me twice as often as he had in the past. And to sate himself.

That was a win.

...wasn't it?

The way he'd licked my clit over my panties had basically turned my brain to mush.

And even though I wanted to keep my power, he was probably going to realize the truth pretty quickly.

"I've only been with a few guys," I admitted. "None of them did this."

His eyes narrowed. "You screwed men who didn't go down on you?"

I nodded.

"Fuckers. Your magic tastes as good as it feels—so it's their loss." He dragged his tongue over the front of my panties again.

My knees trembled as I tried to hold up my weight, but Damian pulled one knee over his shoulder, then leaned me away from the wall. My grip on his hair tightened, and he chuckled, grabbing my other knee and sliding it over his shoulder too.

My core was at his eye level, and my face flushed.

"Perfect." His words were low and gravelly, and his gaze met mine. "You're going to get off on my tongue, little siren. When I bring my fingers in, you'll come again. When I bite you, you'll ride my hand like you did that first day. Understand?"

I was sane enough to nod, though I was too turned on to say anything else.

The way he was taking charge was enough to make me wet.

In one smooth motion, he tore my panties off and tossed

them to the ground, baring my core to him. Then, his mouth was on me.

It was ecstasy.

Pure, unbridled ecstasy.

I came faster than I ever had before, crying out desperately. As he'd promised, he filled me with two of his fingers as I came down from my high, still working me with his tongue.

My cries were louder and more desperate when I lost it that time.

But he didn't stop there.

He just feasted.

Licking.

Sucking.

Biting.

Teasing.

It felt endless—and I hoped like hell it really would be.

I came again, and again, before he finally sank his fangs into my upper thigh and slowly worked my clit with his thumb. Though he gave me a break from the intensity of his mouth, his magic took me higher and higher.

When my desperation finally took hold, I pushed his head and he released my thigh. There was satisfaction in his gaze, but I wasn't done with him.

And, I realized as he set me back down on my feet with his hand still inside me, he wasn't done with me either.

"Has anyone ever fucked you against a wall, little siren?" There was a wicked gleam in his eyes.

"No."

I'd only ever had missionary-style sex before he screwed me in that hospital room.

"Good." He tugged my t-shirt over my head with his free hand, baring my chest before he caught one of my tits and dragged his tongue over my nipple. "Fuck, I love these."

"Thought they were too little," I breathed, and he bit down hard enough to make my hips jerk against his hand.

His rumbly chuckle made me smile, despite my intense need. "You desperate for me already?"

"Never."

"You won't mind if I take my time, then." He sucked my nipple painfully slow.

Impatience struck, and I unbuttoned his jeans for him.

He laughed, biting down again so my hips arched against his palm.

"I need you *now*," I said.

"You know how to get what you need."

He wanted me to use my magic.

"Nice try, but I know you're not sated."

"Clever little siren." He brushed his mouth over my throat, and helped me push his jeans down. When he stepped out of them, I finally got his cock in my hand and bit back a groan at the feel of his thick, silky length.

"I want this in my mouth," I breathed, as his fangs brushed my throat again and he slid his fingers out of my channel.

"You'll have to catch me off guard if you want that kind of control over me."

"Or use my magic."

"Not tonight. Tonight, you wear my release inside your sweet little body."

He finally sank his teeth into my throat, pinning one of my hands above my head as he filled me smoothly.

I nearly forgot how to breathe with the overwhelm of his magic and his cock flooding me.

He thrust inside me as he drank, fucking me slow and deep against the wall until his fangs retracted. I finally let myself dig into his emotions, and the feel of *everything* heightened.

His tongue dragged over the spot he'd bitten me, and I came so hard, I screamed.

He snarled in satisfaction as he drove into me rougher, dragging out my pleasure and filling me with his.

Our chests rose and fell together as we came down from the high.

"That was amazing," I breathed against him.

"You come so fucking well on my mouth."

"Apparently, I like oral sex."

"More proof that you were made for me. I could spend all night between your thighs."

"It felt like you *did*."

He scooped me up and carried me to the bed, grabbing his phone. "Luckily, you tried to go to sleep ridiculously early. We're only fifteen minutes late for the meeting."

"Fifteen minutes? We're not even dressed. Or clean. And you're covered in glitter."

His lips curved wickedly. "Guess there's no time to shower."

"You did this on purpose," I hissed, sliding off his cock. I missed the feel of him immediately, but had to ignore that.

"Of course I did."

I huffed. "I hope they make fun of you for sparkling. What do you wear to these meetings?"

"Clothes."

I flashed him a glare.

He chuckled. "There's no dress code. I usually just wear jeans and a button-up. Bane wears sweats. It's whatever you're comfortable in."

"So I should go with my white bikini?"

His eyes gleamed. "If you don't want me to let you out of the room, sure."

I scowled, stepping into the closet and grabbing a pair of panties and a bra. I didn't have much as far as dress clothing went—didn't have anything, actually—so the only real option was jeans and a fitted tee.

I put them on, and Damian stepped up behind me, moving his hands slowly over the curve of my waist. "You look perfect."

He'd pulled on the same thing he was wearing earlier. "So do you."

My words were a little reluctant. I didn't love admitting how good he looked—mostly because I didn't want him to think he had any more power over me than we both knew he already held.

After I straightened my top, he took my hand and wove his fingers between mine. We took the elevator to the bottom floor, and my hand tightened a little in his.

Meeting the other kings was a big deal. They were powerful men, and they could hurt me if they wanted to. I needed to look strong when we faced them, not like Damian's *little siren*.

"Don't act like we're a real couple in there. We're just mates who are feeding each other and screwing," I warned.

"As opposed to real couples, who are..." he trailed off, waiting for me to fill in the blank.

"In love."

"Ah."

"Exactly."

His playfulness faded as we got closer to the hallway that led into the neutral building between the other wings of the Manor. "I need you to call me Hale while we're around them," he said.

"Alright. You use my name, too."

"Agreed. When they ask, you tell them you don't have any sisters," he added.

I frowned. "Curtis knows how many of us there are."

"Yes, and the rest of them will know he's telling the truth. But as soon as we admit we have four unmated sirens, they will want to start bargaining for one of their own. And we're not bargaining, are we?"

"Hell no."

"Exactly."

"Alright. Anything else?"

He stopped, right before we reached the doors. There was hesitation in his gaze, and something told me I needed to wait and let him decide to tell me whatever he was thinking.

Finally, he said, "I know we refuse to let people call us kings, but deep down, we all know that we are. And wearing my mark makes you my equal, Blair. My queen. Don't let them talk down to you. Don't look away when they challenge you. And please, try to act like you don't hate me."

As much as I didn't want to admit it, whatever I felt for him had veered away from hatred, if it had ever truly been that.

Our conversation in the club that first day had all but guaranteed that I couldn't truly despise him. He had protected me and helped me. Even if it led to him forcing me to be his mate.

And anyway, I wouldn't have been starving for him if I hated him.

I sighed. "You *want* us to act like a real couple, don't you?"

He hesitated, but after a moment, dipped his head.

"Is it the best way to keep my sisters alive?"

"Without question."

"Then for the meeting, we're in love."

His lips curved upward. "Good girl."

"If you ever say that to me in public, I will kick you in the balls and smile when you collapse."

He let out a booming laugh, recapturing my hand and lacing his fingers through mine. "Fuck, you're fun."

"For now."

The grin he gave me was scorching.

And I couldn't fight a smile of my own.

WHEN WE WALKED into the meeting with tangled hair and rumpled clothes, smelling the way we did and equally dusted with glitter, there was no question why we'd been late.

The room it was held in was basically a big lounge, with five couches set up in a circle and a gigantic coffee table between them. There was a bookshelf off to the side of the room, and a few large decorative chairs placed strategically around the massive space to prevent it from feeling messy.

There were four men in the room already. All of them were massive, and all of them were gorgeous.

Even Curtis.

I swear, that room alone held a man for every kind of woman.

Curtis was tall and tan, with curly white-blond hair. Before you got to know him, he was probably the most appealing of the bunch. There was something earthy about were-wolves that was just really, intensely sexy.

At the moment, Curtis was sprawled out over one of the couches, his jaw clenched with anger and his gaze fixed on me.

I'd never looked closely at pictures of the leaders, hence my failure to recognize Damian in the nightclub, but different types of magical beings carried themselves differently. That made it easy enough to tell them apart, paired with my faint memories of the pictures I had seen in the past.

"Couldn't wait to fuck your female until after we were done?" one of the men drawled.

I was pretty sure the one who spoke was Kai, the fae leader. He had light skin and blond hair that was swept up off his face, and he was leaning against the armrest of another couch.

Something told me that the men knew exactly which couch belonged to which king, even if there was no outward sign declaring it.

"That should be *my* female," Curtis growled.

"They've both got permanent mate marks, so I don't know how you're going to prove that," one of the guys said. All of them were monstrous, but that one in particular was built like a tank.

He had the broadest shoulders, the biggest muscles, and the harshest lines on his face. His sun-tanned skin and shaggy, wavy hair contrasted that, so I wasn't sure what to think about him.

Still, his physique alone was enough to say that he was clearly the leader of the monsters. Bane.

He was sitting comfortably on his own couch, his arms draped over the back of it.

Damian released my hand and set his on the small of my back, leading me toward the couch nearest to the door we'd entered through. As we walked, he introduced me.

"Everyone, this is my blood mate, Blair. Blair, you've had the misfortune of meeting Curt already. That's Kai," he gestured to the blond guy, whose name I'd guessed correctly. "That's Bane," he pointed to the wavy-haired guy, so I was right about that one too, "And that's Talon."

Talon was nearly as big as Bane, with light brown skin and black hair that fell to his cheekbones in loose, messy curls. He stood behind his couch, his grip tight on the back of it. "How many sisters does she have?"

"She has a voice, Talon," Damian said, as we sat down on the couch.

"I don't have any sisters. My pod was killed about ten years ago," I explained.

It was half true.

Talon scowled.

Curtis growled. "You know damn well that she has four unmated sisters. Enough to share with the rest of us. One of them wears my mark."

"If you really managed to *lose* the female with your mark on her throat, which magically leads you to her, I think she deserves her freedom," Kai drawled. "What are we really here to talk about?"

"The fact that Curt has attempted to declare war on the vampires by setting up an ambush of wolves at my blood mate's house," Damian said simply.

All three of the other men's gazes moved to Curtis.

Kai looked amused.

Talon looked concerned.

Bane looked pissed.

"I wasn't trying to take your female. I wanted *mine*."

"Security camera footage proves that none of the women at the scene had a band around their neck except Blair." Damian typed on his phone for a moment, and showed me a fairly clear picture from a security camera that definitely hadn't been there before we moved to the Manor. The notifications dinging and buzzing on the other men's phones told me they'd all received it in a message.

They all pulled their devices out and looked at the picture.

"And these women are three of her sisters?" Kai asked dryly.

"Yes," Curtis confirmed, at the same time Damian said, "No. They're three of my vampires."

"Whoever they are, they clearly don't have mate marks," Bane said. "Which makes attacking them an act of war."

He looked back at Curtis.

Kai did too.

Talon was studying the screen closely. A little *too* closely for my comfort.

"I don't want war," Curtis growled. "I want—"

"If you had any right to the woman, you'd have a band around your neck like Hale does. Issue an apology, or go to war with the rest of us," Talon said flatly, his focus still on his phone's screen.

Curtis's face turned beet red. He stood furiously. "I *will* get my female back."

Bane growled, the sound far more menacing than the wolf's.

Curt's red face went a little purple. "But until I do, I apologize for attacking your blood mate."

"Ten vials of blood enhancement were used to heal injuries after the fight," Damian said smoothly. "You'll pay to replace those, as well as my mate's business equipment and personal items, which your wolves destroyed."

"There weren't even ten—"

"Is this really worth a fight, Curt?" Kai asked.

"Fine," Curtis bit out. "I'll have them sent over."

"You'll send the *money* over," Damian corrected. "We have no reason to trust drugs sent by your people at this time."

Curtis snarled, "You'll get your money by the end of the day tomorrow. And I *will* get Clementine back."

He stalked out of the room, and despite the ridiculousness of his words, I *was* a little worried.

His bark might not have mattered, but his bite was dangerous. There were a lot of werewolves. Far more than there were monsters or dragons. They were even with the vampires, but no one knew how many fae there were.

"One of your sisters is named after tiny oranges?" Kai asked, looking at me with a lifted eyebrow.

"I don't have any sisters," I reminded him.

His lips quirked upward. "Right."

"I need a siren," Talon said, finally looking up from his phone screen and straight at me. "I'll take the dark-haired one. I can return her when I'm done."

"If we had extra unmated sirens, which we don't, do you really think we would *loan them out?*" Damian drawled.

Bane interrupted before Talon could growl at us. "If you have a real need and an offer, you can write it out and send it to Hale's office."

Talon scowled. "I'm not wasting time with *paperwork* when I know he's not going to do a damn thing about it. I need a fucking siren."

Kai finally slid off the armrest and sat down on his couch. "If you have a problem, tell us what it is, and we'll see what we can do to help."

Talon hesitated for a moment, then finally shook his head.

Without another word, he left the room the same way Curtis had.

Something told me that wasn't the last we'd hear about his request to *borrow* a siren, and nerves had my stomach tensing. I'd need to warn my sisters to be more careful... but then again, they were already insanely cautious. I wasn't sure we could *get* any more careful.

"Well, that's a little terrifying," Kai remarked. "Glad I'm not the bastard trying to protect four unmated sirens."

"No kidding," Bane rumbled. "I have a hard enough time protecting my females."

Female monsters were rare, so as far as I knew, all of them were housed in his wing of the Manor. He wasn't known for being a nice guy, but monsters did protect their women viciously.

Then again, compared to the humans, we were *all* monsters.

"If I was protecting them, I think I'd just build a really great pool to seduce them into staying safe to make things easy for myself," Damian remarked.

I smacked him on the chest with the back of my hand, and he grinned.

"How's life without bloodlust?" Kai asked.

"Really fucking peaceful, minus the wolves."

"Let us know if you need backup with that. You know we'll intervene if we have to, even before war's officially declared."

"I'll keep it in mind, but I've got something up my sleeve. How's the fae realm?"

Kai grimaced. "Not great. We're going through another eclipse. I can't figure out what's triggering it."

I frowned, not sure what that meant.

Damian squeezed my hip lightly, and I realized his arm was around my waist. "When the fae realm is eclipsed, they're reduced to their most animalistic states. There's a lot of destruction. Death, too."

"Even the earthside fae can feel a weaker version of the effects," Kai added, and I appreciated that they were explaining it to me. "Uncontrollable lust and violence are the most common symptoms in this realm."

"And you think something causes it?"

"Theoretically. It never used to happen this often."

"Hmm."

"It's a shitshow, but we'll pull through," Kai said. "How are the monsters?"

"Solid." Bane nodded. "We're in a better place than we've been in a long time, but that doesn't mean one errant demon can't screw it up at any moment."

The nature of monsters was just plain messy.

They were wildcards, and I was really glad I didn't have to deal with that.

The men continued chatting. Though they mostly talked about their people, they occasionally asked me questions about how I'd grown up. I answered them without bringing my sisters into it, and could see the approval in all of their eyes.

Especially Damian's.

By the time we left, I was thoroughly exhausted... and ready to go home.

Which, strangely enough, had become the room I shared with the vampire king.

fifteen

BLAIR

ON THE WAY HOME, Damian proposed getting rid of the pillow between us in our bed, but I shot that down. He didn't seem surprised by my refusal.

The next day was Wednesday, so he was supposed to feed on me again, but I didn't think he'd go through with it. Considering he'd fed the night before, I figured he deserved a free pass for that one.

I wasn't quite sure how to act around him, given the change between us, so I woke up early the way I had been. After a long swim, I headed down to join my sisters at breakfast. Without my hunger forcing my magic to radiate everywhere, I could interact with the vampires again without having to fight or worry.

That was nice, even if my uncertainty wasn't.

I put in my breakfast order and sat down next to Zora. She was the only one up and moving yet, as far as I could tell, but that didn't surprise me. She was always the first awake, and used to make breakfast for everyone.

We'd reopened our online stores over the past few days as our new equipment came in, so we'd stayed pretty busy, which was nice.

But I couldn't focus on the shops, or what I needed to work on that day.

Everything I'd done the night before kept running through my mind, keeping me wide awake.

My heart beat irrationally fast every time I thought about the way Damian's mouth had felt between my thighs.

"You look cheerful," Zora remarked, as my phone buzzed.

I ignored the device, biting back a smile. "We figured things out last night."

She sighed. "So he's really here to stay?"

"Mmhm. No getting rid of this." I tapped the band around my neck lightly, and she studied it for a moment before nodding.

"I'll try not to hate him so much."

My lips curved. "Don't try to pretend that gorgeous pool hasn't already softened you toward him."

"I will admit to nothing," she vowed, though I could see a touch of humor in her gaze.

Her immediate hatred for him had faded around the time I explained my plan to force him to drink my blood regularly.

Learning that he'd been starving for so long to prevent himself from accidentally killing people humanized him to my sisters, I guess.

They still hadn't fully integrated with the vampires, but they were trying. And I appreciated that.

My phone buzzed again, and I finally flipped it over so I could see the screen.

> DAMIAN
>
> Where are you?
>
> I woke up wanting to sink my teeth into you, little siren

My toes curled.

My body warmed, too.

Zora read the texts over my shoulder, just as snoopy as always.

She was still reading when the third message came in.

> DAMIAN
>
> Remember my promise in the throne room? I think it's fair for that to apply every time you hide from me like this

Excitement made my abdomen tense.

"What did he promise?" she asked.

"That he was going to bite me whenever he wanted."

Her eyebrows lifted.

"He's turning it into a game," I said, rising to my feet. "I have to find somewhere to hide. Can you watch my food for me? I probably won't be back before it—"

I *felt* the man's presence before I saw him.

My gaze met his across the room a heartbeat before his hands were on my waist, walking me backward until my ass met the edge of the table. His teeth slid into my throat, and I gripped the collar of his button-down desperately as I fought the lust flooding through me with his magic.

He was so much more powerful when he bit me after feeding the day before.

His magic was nearly impossible to ignore.

"Fuck you," I breathed, gripping his shirt even harder.

Eyes all around the room were on us.

There was a reason vampires were provided with private rooms when out in public. Watching one feed could most definitely trigger other people's predatorial instincts. Seeing him bite me would push others to want to do exactly the same.

But considering his power level, I didn't imagine anyone would actually lose control of themselves to that level.

Hopefully.

Fingers and toes crossed.

He didn't drink from me for nearly as long as he had the night before when his fangs finally retracted.

My chest rose and fell quickly, pressed against his.

"Everyone's staring at us, huh?" I whispered.

"Yup," Zora said from beside me. She was still sitting down, sprawled out, but there was something bright in her eyes that made me smile.

She was exactly the kind of woman who would love a game like the one Damian had just started.

And it *was* a game. Because he'd just drank from me in the middle of the damn dining room, and I wasn't going to let him get away with that easily.

"Good morning, little siren," Damian said, his eyes bright and his gaze victorious. "Don't leave my bed without waking me up again."

"*Your* bed?" I drawled, though I wasn't offended in the slightest.

I was too damn excited.

"Our bed," he corrected himself, finally taking a step back and sitting down in the chair on the other side of mine.

Our food got there just as I took my seat again, and Damian put in a breakfast order of his own. His hand landed on my thigh under the table, and I bit my lip to hide my stupid smile.

My phone buzzed again, and a glance at the screen made me snort.

The Vamp Manor Homies chat was exploding, but I didn't bother opening it. It would just have more *Big Daddy Hale* and *Big Mama B* shit.

Those weren't the messages that I tapped on.

Zora read over my shoulder again as I opened my conversation with Kara and Lou.

> **KARA**
>
> Looks like Operation Feed a Starving Vampire is a raging success
>
> Victoryyy
>
> **LOU**
>
> He looks so healthy, Blair
>
> You're my new favorite sibling <3

Zora snorted, and I swiped the messages off the screen before Damian could read them.

So, he plucked my phone from my hand and typed the code in to open the messages himself.

"Who told you my password?" I asked.

"I watched you type it in one day. You're not sneaky," he said, going back through my messages with Kara and Lou and shaking his head as he did. "I should tear into them."

"But you won't." I let him have my phone, figuring he couldn't do any real damage as I finally started to eat.

He gave it back a minute later, relaxing in his chair as Zora asked him,

"Any updates on the Curtis situation?"

"Nothing concrete. I'm trying to get in touch with an old friend who could help, but he hasn't gotten back to me yet. Curtis still wants Clementine, but the rest of the leaders are on our side. Publicly and politically, there's nothing he can do to get her back."

"But..." Zora prodded.

"But our people have found far too many of his wolves around the grounds of our wing of the Manor to think he's given up. He's waiting for an opportunity to strike. We have to move against him first."

"He definitely didn't seem like he was going to give up yesterday," I agreed.

Zora asked what I meant, and I gave her a rundown of my meeting with the rest of the leaders.

As we were finishing up breakfast, Clementine finally made it into the room, bleary-eyed but smiling. She plopped down in the seat beside Zora's and leaned over.

"Are we feeding on people in the dining hall now?" she teased, showing me a picture someone had sent in the Homies group.

"If we're the strongest vampire in the room, we are," Damian said, glancing at the photo. He looked a little annoyed, but I knew he didn't appreciate the group conversation or whoever ran it.

Though he didn't like it, even I had realized that it changed the vibes in Vamp Manor. People could talk without hiding that they were gossiping, and it made everyone feel more comfortable.

And *Big Daddy Hale* wasn't the most respectful of names, but it was overwhelmingly clear that everyone who lived there did respect him.

"What if you're the strongest siren in the room?" Zora countered.

"You'd have to have a way to prove it," Damian said with a shrug. "And something tells me you're not about to fight each other for the top ranking."

Zora eyed us like she was considering it, and I snorted. Clementine laughed.

Damian's food arrived, and Clem eyed it hungrily.

He noticed, and after a moment, pushed it across the table for her. "I'll take yours."

"If Blair hadn't already taken you off the market, I'd totally mate you for this," she promised, cutting into the food immediately.

I rolled my eyes, and Zora snorted.

Damian's hand lingered on my thigh as Zora told Clem about my meeting with the leaders.

I listened a little, but mostly, I focused on fighting like hell not to let myself feel way too good about how our morning was going.

I was *not* going to develop feelings for my vampire.

WAKING up with Damian the following day wasn't nearly as weird as I'd imagined. It was actually nice.

...especially when he went down on me to keep me in bed a little longer.

I was still dazed from the orgasms he'd given me, without letting me reciprocate, when we made our way down to breakfast together.

The day after that was another feeding day.

I considered getting up early again to continue our game, but decided to wait and see if he brought it up. Because if he was offering to bite me after he had his tongue on me again, I'd abandon the game in a heartbeat.

He ate me out in our bed again that morning, but his fangs didn't make an appearance when he did.

And he got me off too many times to be disappointed about the lack of teeth.

We had breakfast, then parted ways again so we could work separately. An idea struck me, and I couldn't fight my grin throughout the day as I handled our online store stuff with my sisters.

They noticed, and when I told them my plan, had various reactions of amusement.

None of them were as excited as I was, but that didn't bug me. They weren't the ones going head-to-head with a big, gorgeous vampire.

I had dinner with Damian like usual that night, and told him I had a little more work to do afterward. His eyes narrowed, but he didn't try to stop me as I headed back in the direction of the room my sisters and I had been given for our online store things.

He'd promised to hunt me down if I wasn't in our room when he went to bed, and I was totally going to use that.

As soon as I was out of his sight, I headed in the opposite direction from our workroom, hurrying straight for the pool.

There were a few vampires floating and swimming, but that would work in my favor.

I stripped off all my clothes—ignoring the catcalls and whistles—and called out, "If anyone tells Hale where I am before he finds me himself, I'm hiding my underwear in your room and setting him loose on you."

Grins and laughter followed the promise.

I didn't know them individually, but I trusted them to keep it a secret just until Damian found me himself. Messages had already gone around about our game after someone overheard me telling Zora about it the other morning.

Diving in, I swam to the bottom of the pool and tucked myself away in a little cove as far from the surface as you could get. I knew Damian could hold his breath long enough to get to the bottom—but if he didn't see me right away, I could totally win the game.

If there really *was* a winner.

Was it even a game if no one won?

I decided I didn't care. It was fun, regardless.

So, I relaxed in the pool, and waited.

My excitement rose higher the more time passed.

Two or three hours must've gone by when I finally saw a familiar pair of thick arms—and a set of electric blue eyes.

Damian was just as naked as I was.

The bastard must've cleared out the pool. I couldn't help but grin at the realization.

He darted toward my cove, and at the last moment, I shot away.

Laughter cut through me as he chased me for a minute, but had to go back to the surface for air.

Oh, the man was going to be *furious.*

My smile stretched wider.

I watched the surface of the water, frowning when I didn't see him dive back down again. He actually got out of the pool for some reason.

My eyes tracked the surface.

A solid minute had gone by when I realized there was another entrance. It was on the other side of a massive rock wall that connected to the main part with a tunnel. He could go through that, and—

I screeched into the water when he grabbed me from behind, his victorious laughter bubbling up to my ears as he carried me back to the surface. We'd barely broken through the water when his teeth were in my throat, one of his hands on the ledge behind me and the other grabbing one of my thighs. He opened me up and drove into me as he drank.

I held onto his shoulders for dear life as he screwed me in the pool, bringing new sensations to life for me.

Water was just blissful.

And Damian was really, really good at sex.

I was coming hard by the time his fangs retracted and he lost control with me, filling me with his pleasure.

My bare chest rose and fell against his as we recovered, and for once, he didn't lecture me about getting naked in public.

He just kissed me.

And fucked me again, slower and sweeter, while his tongue moved with mine.

It was surreal.

And so, so good.

When we came together again, I pressed my face against his neck, and he held me close. His hand moved slowly over my back, and I fought a sigh at how amazing it felt.

"You're not going to yell at me for stripping?" I teased, my voice soft after the intimacy of the moments we'd shared.

Sex in the water was definitely a new favorite.

"Nah. I figure I'll just start walking around naked whenever you do."

My eyes widened against his neck. "What?"

"You know I get texts when you strip, right? I might be an asshole, but I'm a good leader. My people report that shit to me."

"I guess that makes sense…"

"So, next time I get a text that my mate has stripped, I'll just drop my clothes wherever I'm at so we can both be walking around naked."

My eyes widened further.

I couldn't help but imagine Damian stripping down in the dining room, while Missy and everyone else who lusted after the big, sexy bastard drooled.

I couldn't stop myself from growling a little. "No."

"No?" He feigned surprise. "You love public nudity, little siren."

"You're not stripping in front of anyone but me," I grumbled. "I'll stop swimming naked."

"You can still swim naked," he said, playing with my hair lightly. "After I've cleared the pool for you, and when there's no one in here but me."

"That's fair, I guess."

"Finally, she sees reason."

I elbowed him in the gut, and he laughed, making his cock jerk where he was still buried inside me.

"You like our game, don't you?" he asked me, his voice upbeat.

"It's hard not to like it when it ends like this. Emphasis on *hard*."

He grinned, thrusting his hips and making me bite back a groan. "I'd say we should enjoy it a little longer, but there's supposed to be a movie night in here tonight. I already had them push back the start time, but they're probably getting irritated out there."

My eyes widened. "Shit, I didn't realize."

"I'll buy a round of drinks as a thank you. They won't care."

We slipped out of the water and pulled our clothes back on, then opened the nearest door to let everyone in.

They were all friendly, and chatted normally as they filed into the room. The group was much bigger than I would've expected.

"Thanks for letting us take over tonight," the final guy inside said with a grin. I thought he was talking to Damian at first, but realized after a minute that he was speaking to me. "I was worried we wouldn't get approved for a minute."

"Oh, you should thank Hale." I patted him lightly on the chest. "It's his pool."

The guy snorted. "You're the one feeding him—you can claim anything that's his. You've got him by the balls, Blair." He smacked Damian on the arm before jogging over to the pool and diving in.

"Hey, lovebirds," a woman called out from the pool. When I looked over at her, I realized she was the woman I'd met the first time I went swimming. Missy's sister. The one who was dating Roscoe. "Go put your swimsuits on and come join us! Movie starts in twenty minutes, after we get the drinks going around!"

"We'll think about it," I called back, irritation striking me with the title she'd used.

We weren't *lovebirds*.

We were just two people who fed each other.

And screwed.

And shared a room.

And had a mate bond.

But that didn't mean there were feelings involved.

Damian took my hand and led me down the hallway, toward the elevator that led up to our room.

He tucked me up against his chest, resting his chin on my head as the elevator carried us upward. After a moment of silence, he asked, "Do you want to go to the movie night?"

"I don't know. I've never been to something like that."

He was quiet, and I had the feeling he was considering it.

Finally, he said, "Do you think your sisters will ever take mates?"

The question caught me off guard. "I haven't ever considered it."

"They can't meet anyone outside the Manor right now, but after we've figured out a way to make peace with Curtis, they'll be free to come and go as they please. They'll obviously still need to be careful, but I can't imagine they're going to stay here all the time."

I frowned. "I guess if they could interact with the rest of society with vampires there to protect them, I can see a few of them eventually falling in love. I know Izzy's already itching to get out of the Manor, so... yeah. I think they'll eventually take mates, if just for the protection."

"When that happens, you'll have an easier time with it if you have friends here. Because I won't let you go." His arm was around my waist, his casual grip was so completely opposite of the certainty in his voice.

"I guess," I admitted.

I was already friends with Lou and Kara, but they both had

other friends. I'd need people to share meals with, other than Damian. People to swim with from time to time.

"Then I think we should go to the movie night," he said. "It could be a good start to that."

"Alright," I agreed. "I'll befriend a few vampires."

"You've already got one." He nudged the side of my throat with his nose.

"Lou?" I teased, as the elevator dinged with its arrival.

He whisked me off my feet and ran me to the bed, tossing me onto the mattress just to make me laugh.

"I'm picking your swimsuit," he said, as he strode into the closet.

"Pick the pink bikini." It was the skimpiest one I owned, though a few of my sisters had some far skimpier ones.

"I'd sooner burn it," he called back.

I couldn't fight my grin.

Damian picked out my bathing suit while I sent a message to my sisters to let them know about the movie night in case they were interested. I tossed my phone onto our bed when I was done, deciding to do my best to make some friends.

I was going to spend my life at Vamp Manor for better or worse, so it was time to make it a little better.

sixteen

BLAIR

WE MADE it back to the pool fairly quickly. I was wearing one of my one-piece swimsuits, thanks to a certain possessive vampire asshole, but I didn't mind.

After our conversation about nudity earlier, I was trying to see things from his perspective, and I understood enough to play along.

The movie had started and the drinks were distributed when we got there. We made ourselves comfortable on the far side of the pool, tucked in a small gap between two floating tubes. Our butts were on the rock and our feet in the water.

My back was pressed comfortably against Damian's front as we sat, his arm securely around my middle. Someone passed me a fruity cocktail, and I took a sip, lifting my eyebrows at the flavor.

"I don't drink very often, but that's pretty good," I remarked. "Try it." I passed the glass to Damian, and he took a sip, nodding and handing it back.

"You hate it, don't you?" I teased.

His lips quirked upward. "Not my favorite."

"If they give you one, I want it."

"Deal." He pressed a kiss to the side of my throat, his lips brushing the sensitive mate mark there.

Sure enough, he was given a drink a few minutes later, and it became mine too.

Alcohol didn't affect magical beings very much, but that didn't mean we couldn't have fun drinking it.

The movie was a rom-com that made me laugh a few times, and the intermittent chatter around us was really comfortable. Being surrounded by my sisters all the time meant I was used to that easy-going camaraderie, and many of Damian's vampires seemed to share it.

So it made me feel like I was home.

Then again, the big, strong arm around my waist might've made a difference too.

When the movie ended, I thought everyone would split up... but someone turned on some music instead.

All of the inner tubes and other floatation devices were tossed out, and the guy who'd greeted us at the door announced loudly that it was time for Sharks and Minnows.

"What's that?" I whispered to Damian.

He summed up the rules of the game—a big group of "minnows" swam across the pool while a small group of "sharks" tried to tag them, turning them into sharks too.

"We want Blair," the first shark announced, and groans echoed through the room as a bunch of people looked at me.

"We get Hale, then," the first minnow announced.

That didn't cheer them up.

I bit back a smile and pushed Damian's arms off my waist, diving in and swimming out to join the other two sharks.

Everyone lined up, and my gaze caught on my mate's.

He was watching me closely, daring me to take him down.

"Here's the plan," the first shark guy said, and me and the other girl turned toward him. "I take Hale. You know he's going to try to distract you, Blair."

I nodded.

That much was already clear.

"No strategizing!" one of the minnows exclaimed.

The guy gave me a nod that I probably should've understood the meaning of.

I nodded back, even though I wasn't entirely sure what he was trying to say.

Either way, I had to resist the urge to go after Damian.

Someone yelled, "GO!" and the game began.

There were bodies everywhere.

Arms and legs kicking, swimming clumsily but with everything they had. And with vampire speed, they had plenty.

But I had the same speed.

I sailed through the water, tagging, then tugging on ankles when they ignored being tagged.

Splashes, protests, and laughter echoed through the room, bringing the pool to life even more.

Damian was the last minnow standing, facing off against all of us with a ferocious grin.

He'd been drinking from me enough that he seemed to be tapping into his enhanced speed without even realizing it.

And he was faster than me—faster than all of us—but I had a trick up my sleeve.

I made eye contact with the first shark guy and mouthed, *distract him.*

The guy grinned, then yelled at Damian, "You're moving faster than a vampire is supposed to!"

"It's not my fault you're a bunch of slow fuckers," my mate tossed back, as I sank slowly beneath the water.

I'd have to be careful about what I was going to do, because it could go wrong fairly easily.

My magic wasn't exactly stable. I was already a little hungry. I'd noticed Damian trying to keep me away from other people the day before, so I could tell my magic was radiating a little.

But I couldn't drink from him yet because of our agreement.

So, the hunger remained.

I was just going to make it work in my favor, for once.

I slowly glided across the pool, heading toward the edge, and focused on the feel of the water. I couldn't control it, but if I paid attention, I could feel exactly how and when it moved.

At the first sign of Damian's motion, I pushed my magic to the surface, focused completely on drawing him in.

He was on me in a heartbeat, colliding with me and swimming me deeper into the water as I released my hold on my magic. The water dissipated it smoothly, and I crossed my fingers that no one else had time to feel it.

We surfaced a moment later, and I laughed as whoops and cheers erupted through the room so loudly my ears rang.

"Cheater," Damian said with a grin. There was no heat behind the accusation—he actually looked kind of proud.

"If you get to use your magic, so do I," I tossed back.

"She could wipe the floor with all of us if she tried," the first shark guy declared, swimming up to us and tossing his arm over my shoulder.

Damian's eyes narrowed at him, and he quickly removed it.

"Don't touch Big Mama B if you like having hands," someone called from across the room."

Damian made a noise of exasperation, but I laughed so hard that my eyes watered.

"Is there room for us in there?" Clementine called out, approaching the edge of the pool with the rest of my sisters. Izzy seemed reluctant, but the rest of them actually looked excited.

"Hell yeah!" the shark guy said, gesturing for them to get in. "I think we need the sirens to play minnows while the rest of us are sharks."

My sisters all jumped in, heading for the wall when they were pointed that way.

"Someone has to teach us how this works so we can kick your asses," Zora announced, and someone launched into another explanation.

"Go to the wall, little siren," Damian said, a wicked gleam in his eyes as he shooed me toward the minnows' starting point.

I was totally going to lose...

But I'd have a blast doing it.

OUR POOL CREW ended up in the dining hall around two AM, feasting on ice cream from a soft serve machine that I'd foolishly never visited before. Everyone was spread out across different tables, and though we were sitting with my sisters, we were still interacting with the other vampires a lot more than we usually did.

"We need one of these machines in our room," I told Damian, my legs draped over his lap as I relaxed in the chair next to his.

"We need one in one of *our* rooms," Zora corrected. "Maybe we can come up with a way to make it a tax write-off."

"Ice cream?" Avery asked, lifting an eyebrow. "Seems like a stretch."

"It can be our mental-health soft serve machine," Zora said, biting into her fourth or fifth cone. Luckily, someone in our group had a key to the place they kept the machine's refills.

"Ice cream is good for the soul," Clementine agreed.

"Someone better talk to our government about that." Zora fixed her eyes on me.

I laughed. "My connections aren't *that* good."

She looked at Damian.

Everyone else did too. Except Izzy; she was keeping to herself and still looked a little uncomfortable.

"Her connections *are* that good. Write it off," Damian said with a shrug.

"Blair totally took one for the team when she mated with you," Zora said.

I glanced at him, worried he'd find that offensive, but he just chuckled. "You aren't wrong."

We ate ice cream and chatted for another half an hour before people started peeling away from the group, finally heading to bed.

"Same time next week?" the shark guy called out, his gaze on me (I finally learned that his name was Colby).

"Ask him," I called back, gesturing to Damian.

"It's your pool," Damian countered, looking at me. "One of my assistants already set up a calendar for you. I only agreed to tonight because Colby hunted me down and refused to take no for an answer."

My protesting hadn't achieved a damn thing, and I did kind of want to know when things were going to happen at the pool... so, I finally called out, "Same time next week."

A few people whooped, and there was satisfaction in Damian's eyes.

"I'm calling it a night," Izzy announced, standing up.

The rest of my sisters followed suit. A few of them looked concerned about Iz, but I knew she could take care of herself. Whatever she was dealing with, she would figure it out.

Their departure left me alone with Damian, but having just the two of us there wasn't uncomfortable the way it would've been before. It wasn't tense, either.

He squeezed one of my feet, since they were still on his lap. "Ready for bed?"

"Mmhm."

Instead of throwing me over his shoulder and speeding us to the elevator like he did fairly often, he offered me a hand as he stood.

When I took it, he pulled me to my feet and tucked me close to his side. The feel of him against me, with his arm draped over my shoulder, put me at ease in a way not even his magic could.

It was natural, and genuine.

And just... *real.*

"I kind of miss your glitter," he remarked, teasing my hair a little.

"It's never returning, so deal with it," I warned, and he chuckled.

We were quiet through the rest of the ride up to our space, but it was nice.

Comfortable.

Easy.

We got back to our room, and Damian kissed the top of my head. "I'm going to take a quick shower."

The pool's water was completely clean, thanks to mine and my sisters' magic, but I could understand wanting to rinse off after being in it with a ton of random people anyway.

I didn't feel the need to wash off, so I just stripped down in the closet and pulled my usual sleep t-shirt over my head. On my way to the bed, I tied my damp hair up in a bun so it wouldn't bug me while I tried to sleep.

As I tucked myself into bed, my eyes moved over Damian's bare back. I watched him scrub his hair with shampoo until I reached the bed and could no longer see him.

The man was gorgeous.

Ridiculously attractive.

Though my gaze lingered on his ass for a moment, that wasn't what I focused on the most.

The mark on the back of his neck took that prize.

My mark.

I'd seen it before, obviously. Every day. And there was no getting around what it meant, but I guess I had never really let it sink in before.

Damian was mine.

There was no going back for him.

He couldn't change his mind, or walk away.

We were mates.

And it wasn't necessarily what I wanted, but there was no getting away from it. No use in pretending we were anything else.

I didn't have to fall in love with him—but I did have to be his partner for the rest of my life, just like he had to be mine.

The bond made us a team.

And that was really, really intense.

I finally looked away from him, biting my lip as I curled up with my pillow on our bed and closed my eyes, trying to sleep.

My breathing evened as I drifted in and out of sleep, hovering on the edge as Damian, my *mate*, dried off and slipped into bed with me.

As he turned toward the pillow, but didn't cross it.

As he brushed a hand lightly over the top of my hair, smoothing a few loose strands away from my face like he didn't want them to bother me.

And in my half-conscious state, I finally admitted to myself that if I had to spend my life with someone, I could've done a lot worse.

seventeen

BLAIR

OUR GAME quickly became one of my favorite parts of my life. Not because of the sex—though that was incredible —but because it was just *fun*.

Damian tried to catch me off guard.

I made him hunt me down.

We both walked away from it grinning, every time.

I tried harder to integrate myself into vampire society, as well. We went to the movie nights in the pool every week, and though my sisters were there, I tried to get to know other people too.

My sisters would always be my sisters, and we would always be close, but I wanted to be part of the community too. Not just as Vamp Manor's *Big Mama B*, or the siren who was mated to the king. But as myself.

So, I socialized.

. . .

THE TIME PASSED QUICKLY.

I realized it had been an entire month since we made our agreement one morning, while I was sitting at breakfast.

Damian wasn't there, but he'd texted me about a video meeting he had with some backwoods vampire clan that morning. So I'd known he wasn't going to make it.

I considered bringing him something to eat, but didn't want to make things weird.

And what if he'd already asked someone to bring him something?

Then again, it wasn't weird when *he* brought *me* food.

It wouldn't hurt just to ask if he'd eaten, would it?

I was eyeing my phone when someone dropped into the empty seat beside mine. I glanced over at the man, offering a smile in greeting.

"Hey, Mama B."

Everyone had started calling me that. It was annoying, in an endearing way. At least they'd dropped the *Big* part. That bit never felt like a compliment.

"Hi, Colby. I remember asking you to call me Blair."

He set his arms on the table, leaning closer to me. He seemed to have learned his lesson about putting an arm over my shoulders when we were in the pool, and hadn't violated my personal space since then. "You haven't replied to my proposition."

My forehead creased.

"I don't think you want that line getting back to her mate," Izzy drawled from the seat beside mine. She didn't seem any more comfortable with the vampires than she'd been a month earlier, even though the rest of my sisters had all made friends and settled in.

"Hale knows I'm not after his woman. He's the one who sent me to talk to her," Colby clarified. "It's a *pool* proposition."

I raised my eyebrows.

That was the first time Damian had sent someone to me. Especially someone male. Usually, if an important conversation needed to be had, he was the one who would talk to me.

"I sent you a request about using the pool to build some bridges between us and some of the other factions. I'm good friends with a bunch of fae who are suffering through the effects of the eclipse on their land, and water helps them. Because of your magic, and your pool, we've got the best water in the city."

Oh.

Wow.

"I never got a request," I said.

"Hale's office said to submit it to your manor number."

"Manor number?"

"They said they assigned you one."

I bit my lip. "Even if they did, shouldn't that be Hale's decision? Letting fae in seems like something he should decide."

"They would be vetted for connections with the wolves before our security team would let them through, but it's never been a problem in the past," Colby said.

"I'll figure out what's going on with the manor number and talk to Hale. Give me a few hours."

"I'll check in again tomorrow."

Something told me he wasn't going to let it go until I gave him a solid decision. And while I was used to taking a reluctant leadership position where my sisters were concerned, I was absolutely not prepared for it as it applied to Vamp Manor.

He plucked a strawberry off my plate and strode away, saying over his shoulder, "Thanks, Mama B."

"Don't call me that," I called out behind him.

"Your magic's radiating again. Snack on Hale while you're up there," he hollered, loud enough that the entire dining room had to have heard.

One of my sisters snorted, and I ran a hand over the top of my hair, sending a quick text to Damian.

ME

Do I have a manor phone number?

"He's not letting you starve again, is he?" Avery asked me, slightly concerned.

"No, but we still have that agreement. I'm only drinking from him once a week, and the blood booster injections seem to have made me permanently hungrier."

"It makes sense that you'd need more food with your magic working overtime to make more blood," Zora remarked.

"I guess. But I'm reluctant to start a conversation about feeding more when we've managed so long without any real fights," I admitted.

He was still an asshole, but not in a way I couldn't handle. If he'd been much nicer, I would've walked all over him, because I wasn't exactly someone who could just go with the flow.

"I'd put money on someone telling him what Colby just said, so I don't think it'll be a problem much longer," Zora put in.

My phone buzzed.

> **DAMIAN**
>
> Yes. It's connected to the tablet that's been waiting for you on my desk since we sealed our bond

> **ME**
>
> You didn't tell me there was a tablet

> **DAMIAN**
>
> I was waiting for evidence that you were interested in getting involved

Why did I just get dozens of texts about you being hungry?

ME

Colby

DAMIAN

Colby what?

ME

Yelled about it to the crowd

DAMIAN

So your magic isn't radiating?

I'm so attracted to you, I can't tell when it is anymore

I bit my lip and stood up, heading toward one of the doors that led into the kitchen.

ME

It might be

I need to come grab the tablet, and talk to you about Colby's proposition

DAMIAN

Colby's what?

I will fucking kill him

ME

It's a pool proposition

Not a sex one

Just stay in your office. I'll be there in a minute. Did you already have breakfast?

DAMIAN

No, but I'm not hungry anymore

I'm logging into the security cameras as
we speak

I'm rolling my eyes, because there's
nothing sexual about this situation

DAMIAN

Your ass looks good in those jeans

I snorted, putting my phone in my pocket and rolling my eyes at the nearest security camera for good measure.

I made a quick stop in the kitchen. After politely requesting a plate of whatever was cooked and ready at the moment for the king, someone put a tray in my hands, and I headed to the elevator. I'd only been to Damian's office a few times, and never for more than a few minutes, but I wouldn't have a problem finding it.

Damian met me at the elevator on the floor of his office, smoothly taking the tray from my hands. "You didn't need to get me breakfast."

"You bring me food all the time."

"I'm your mate."

"And I'm yours."

"Well, thank you," he said, letting me step into his office in front of him. I noticed that a second desk had been set up in the large room, and frowned.

"You're sharing an office with someone now? Who?"

"You." He set the food down on "my" desk.

I opened drawers, looking for proof that it wasn't actually mine, but didn't find anything. "Why do I need a desk in here?"

"My decorator seems to think you're going to be involved with running my wing of the Manor. She couldn't be convinced otherwise. I think Lou's whispering in her ear. I've just been using it as a table."

He sat down in "my" chair, cutting into his food immediately.

I took his seat, my gaze moving over the mountains and valleys of paperwork. "I'm surprised you guys don't do everything online."

"Almost everything is. These are just the things that have to be printed."

"Like what?"

"Case files I've been sent by the neutral territory's reception desk, formal requests, and documents that have to be signed in person. A lot of them have to do with my nightclubs and other properties."

I picked up a stack and leafed through it, whistling when I saw all the colored tabs indicating where to sign. It looked like a real estate contract of some kind.

"Your tablet is in the top left drawer," he said.

I opened it up, finding an expensive device in a glitter-encrusted case.

"It matches you," he said with a wink.

"Hey, I'm not glittery anymore."

"Just a little. There's still some on your side of the bed. I see it on the backs of your thighs and in your hair sometimes."

"You enjoy that, don't you?"

His lips curved upward. "Immensely."

I smiled, opening the cover on the tablet.

The screen lit up, fully-charged and showing a few dozen notifications. Most were calendar requests, but a handful of them were messages.

"How much am I supposed to be in charge of?" I asked him, skimming the messages and requests.

"Just the pool."

I lifted my gaze to him, raising an eyebrow. "Your vampires wouldn't have given me a desk in the King's office if all I was expected to do was run the pool."

"Historically, a mated leader pair handles everything related to their people together. Equally," he admitted. "But considering the situation, I don't expect that from you. You like the businesses you run with your sisters. I can take care of everything on my own."

"But you did assign me the pool."

"Technically, my activity planner resigned when she learned why I built a pool instead of a monstrous mini-golf course. My assistants are the ones who assigned you the pool and set up the tablet. Convincing them to take it back and put someone else in charge hasn't been a priority."

"The mini-golf course was that important?"

"Not to me."

I grimaced. "Who else resigned when you mated with me?"

"No one irreplaceable."

"Damian," I warned.

"The activity manager, facility manager, and my public relations chairman. Someone else filled the chair, though."

"Was it Colby?" The requests I'd seen from him about using the pool for the fae had been written formally enough for that to seem plausible.

"Unfortunately."

I sighed. "You should've told me this sooner."

"I didn't give you a choice about mating. I wasn't—and am not—going to force you into a leadership role that you don't want just because your blood quiets my lust."

"Do you pay your leaders?"

"Of course."

"Then asking me to take a job is nothing like forcing me to be your mate. I'll talk to my sisters about it, but they really don't need me to run the shops. We only started them because we needed a way to make money, and liked having that independence. I'm sure I can handle running the activities and managing the facility—unless you have someone else doing that already."

"I'm doing it," he said grudgingly.

"Would that help ease some of this?" I gestured to the mountain range of paperwork.

"Tremendously. But..."

"But what?"

He drummed his fingers on my desk, his lips pressing in a line and his breakfast momentarily forgotten. "Both of those roles require interacting with my vampires consistently."

"I thought the goal was for me to get to know people and establish myself here."

"Of course it is."

"Then what's the problem?"

"You're radiating magic."

I sighed. "I can't stop that."

"You can."

"Not without feeding. And last I checked, you didn't want me drinking from anyone but you."

His eyes narrowed. "That will never change."

"Then our problem has a solution. Agree to drink from me six out of seven days, and I'll feed from you twice a week. I won't have to radiate magic anymore, and you won't have to fight your fangs back every other day like you are now. You know you feel much better with our current schedule than you ever did before."

"Your blood was made for me. I don't need as much as I'm already taking," he said, though I could see in his eyes that he didn't believe himself completely anymore.

"Your body was made to drink from me. Frequently."

"Four days a week *is* frequently."

"It's not enough. I can see it in your eyes when you're hungry now, and you're hungry every day."

"I crave you constantly. That doesn't mean I need to drink from you all the time."

"Alright," I said, opening up my messages with the same code I used to get to our room. "What are your assistants' names?"

"Rachel and Rodger."

I found their contacts already programmed in, and sent them both a quick message letting them know about the jobs I'd be taking over.

"What are you doing?" He eyed me suspiciously.

"Messaging our assistants. Looks like they're going to send me the information I need."

He narrowed his eyes. "Not if you're radiating magic."

"Then you're going to have to change our agreement," I said bluntly.

"Stubborn little siren," he growled, rising to his feet.

Though I was significantly shorter than him, I stood too, to even the playing field between us a little. "I'll wear that title with pride."

Damian grabbed my hips, his grip a little rougher than usual. "If you want me to drink from you six days a week, I'm going to need a better deal than the one you're offering. You're trying to control me, and I'm highly aware of it."

"I'm not trying to control you, asshole. I'm trying to take care of you," I bit out. "What do you want?"

His eyes flashed. "I want you feeding on me every time I drink from you."

I scoffed. "No way. If you want me to feed anywhere near that often, you have to drink from me every single day."

"I'll feed six times a week in exchange for feeding you just as often. That's my offer. You can take it or leave it. But if you meet with anyone about the jobs while radiating magic like this, I *will* lock you in our room."

I glared at him, grabbing my tablet off the desk. "Fuck you. I'm *not* your prisoner." I strode out of the room, slamming the door behind me as I headed for the elevator.

Just when I'd started to think he wasn't that much of an asshole, he had to go and do something like that.

Bastard.

. . .

I KNEW my sisters would be working, so I stopped by their rooms to let them know I was going to have to work with the vampires instead of helping them with the shops. None of them seemed surprised or bothered by the news, so at least that went well.

From there, I went up to mine and Damian's room. I hit the button to prevent the elevator from opening on our floor, and twisted the lock that blocked entry to our room from the staircase.

Then, I abandoned my jeans on the floor and curled up in bed with my tablet. Throwing my anger into the reading, I pulled up the information the assistants had sent me about my jobs. I started with the activities one, because I already had those pool requests.

It was a basic instruction book, so I ended up emailing back and forth with them to figure out how security worked, what was allowed, and what wasn't.

IT WAS dinner time when I finally felt like I had a small understanding of what I was allowed to schedule and what I should turn down.

The assistants added me to the activity calendar before they quit for the day, so I scrolled through the massive list of requests.

Damian was clearly overwhelmed with all the work he had done, because some of them were more than a month old.

They hadn't been rejected—they just hadn't been accepted either.

Considering that he had things to do with financial and security impacts, it didn't surprise me that the activities had been at the bottom of his priority list. That was exactly what he should've done.

But it couldn't be ignored indefinitely.

My eyes blurred by the time I finished going through the list. I had to double-check the existing schedule and the rules I'd scrawled out every time I got to a new request. When I had to turn something down, I made sure to add feedback explaining why it wasn't allowed or that it over-lapped with something else that had been planned first.

I was positive I'd piss some people off in the process, but I'd figure it out as I went. And given who my mate was, I couldn't see anyone in the Manor having the balls to attack me for rejecting their activity.

It was nearly midnight when Damian tried to unlock the door leading into the stairwell. My lock prevented it from opening more than a fraction of an inch.

He pushed against it a few times, before my phone rang.

I sent it to voicemail.

He called again.

I sent it to voicemail again.

My anger had faded, but I wasn't letting that bastard in without a sincere and meaningful apology.

He tried to open the door a few more times—then sent me a text.

DAMIAN

Let me in

ME

No.

If you can threaten to lock me in our room, I can damn well lock you out of it.

DAMIAN

I shouldn't have threatened that

Let me in so we can talk

ME

There's nothing to talk about.

DAMIAN

Have you eaten dinner?

I hadn't.

I hadn't had lunch, either.

I'd been too pissed at him to eat in the middle of the day, and too lost in figuring out one of my new jobs to even think about dinner.

My stomach rumbled, but I ignored it.

DAMIAN

It drives me insane to imagine other vampires lusting after you because of your hunger. I feel like your magic should be mine and mine alone. I should've taken a few minutes to calm down instead of arguing with you. I'm sorry.

I blinked down at my phone, reading and then rereading the message.

DAMIAN

> Please open the door. I'd like to have a better conversation about it than the one we had earlier. And you do need to eat. I saw on the security cameras that you've been up here all day.

After letting out a long breath, I set my tablet down on the bed and padded over to the door, undoing the lock and pulling it open. I still didn't have any pants on, but between my top and underwear, I was covered enough not to feel like I was showing too much skin.

He'd already seen it all anyway. So many times.

Damian was leaning against the door's frame, his gorgeous blue eyes dark as they moved up and down my figure like he was making sure I was okay.

"I can't handle knowing that your magic makes other people want you as desperately as I do," he said. "I can't think straight. I'm sorry."

"Do you think it makes me feel good to know that you're weaker than you could be? That if there was an attack, someone could die because you're not at full strength? That *you* could die? We've had enough bullshit around this subject, Damian. A licensed doctor studied your blood to determine how much you need to eat to stay on top of your health, and you refuse to follow her advice."

He dragged a hand through his hair. "I'm fucking terrified of what that will cost me. What it will cost you, too. What if I hurt you? What if I become reliant? What if I get too comfortable and something happens to you?"

"Nothing is going to happen to me. We're mates, remember?" I stepped closer to him, reaching for the mark on his throat.

My mark.

I dragged my fingertips lightly over the length of it, and he let out a slow breath.

"Fear is a normal part of life, Damian. We can't predict the future, and we can't control it either. But there's no point in hiding from it, or living like the worst is just around the corner. If life goes to shit, we'll figure it out together."

"Alright," he said, his eyes meeting mine again. "I'll drink from you every day. No extra requirements or exceptions. But I do want you topping off your magic every time I drink from you."

"That's fair."

The tension in his shoulders eased slightly. "And you need to eat three meals a day, too."

"I usually do, so that's not a problem."

He stepped closer, cupping my cheek in his palm and tilting my head back. "I'm going to bring our food upstairs. Do you have a problem with that?"

"No."

Leaning down, he kissed me lightly. I deepened the kiss, and he pulled me closer. His erection was against my abdomen, but neither of us acted on his clear desire.

When he released me a few minutes later, I was breathing a little faster.

"Don't run or hide from me tonight, little siren."

"I won't."

He kissed me one more time before he left me in our doorway, striding down the stairs.

I watched him go until he turned the next corner, then stepped back into the room. After hitting the button to unlock the elevator, I went back to bed and slipped into the cocoon of blankets I'd formed earlier.

EATING dinner in bed wasn't the most sanitary of decisions, but we threw manners to the wind and did exactly that. While we ate, Damian asked me about the schedule I'd been going through, and helped me figure out what to do with a few things I'd been unsure about.

He promised to teach me how to do my other job the next day, and after we set our dishes on the floor next to our bed, he pulled me into his arms and held me close.

Something about the physical contact was exactly what I needed.

I held him tightly, closing my eyes and breathing in his

scent. Though I was still wearing nothing but my panties and top, there was nothing sexual about the moment.

It was just nice.

Really nice.

"You smell like peppermint," Damian murmured into my hair.

"I've been adding it to my water like it's going out of style."

He chuckled. "It's a nice scent." His hand moved slowly over my back, and we fell quiet for a few minutes before he admitted, "I'm glad you're here with me."

"I am too."

My admission felt big.

Important.

And I wasn't sure how to feel about that.

Thankfully, Damian gave me the best kind of distraction

His lips brushed my ear. "Open your legs for me, little siren."

It was technically a command... but one I wanted to follow.

So, I did.

One of his hands smoothed over my ass and slipped between my thighs, rubbing over my center lightly through my panties. "That feel good?"

"So good," I whispered.

"Open wider."

I followed the order.

His lips brushed my cheek before his fingers finally dipped beneath the hem of the fabric between us, brushing over my wet heat.

I pressed my forehead to his throat a little harder as my hips arched, moving with his hand. He murmured, "Take what you need."

I pulled on his emotions without hesitation.

Lust.

Gratitude.

Devotion.

His magic flooded me as he bit down on my throat, and I sucked in a breath.

If I'd been in my right mind, the intensity of his feelings would've caught me off guard. But with his teeth in my veins and the hunger in my lower belly, I was lost in the ocean of his emotions.

I drank while he touched me, sending my orgasm spiraling through me fast. I cried out in pleasure as I came, my body tightening around nothing.

I wanted him.

Needed him.

When I said as much, he rolled me onto my back, freeing his cock and tugging my panties to the side. He filled me without bothering to remove either of our clothes, and I gasped as he hit every sensitive place inside me like the expert he'd become.

My pleasure rose until we shattered together, and he rolled us back over as we came down from our highs, panting.

He released my throat, licking the sensitive place where he'd bitten me. I let go of my hold on his emotions, insanely sated.

"You like it when I'm in charge, don't you?" He asked, his voice edging on playful again.

I loved it when he got like that.

"Maybe a little," I mumbled.

"Or a lot."

"Maybe."

He chuckled, running his hand slowly down my back. "Do you want to watch a movie or something? I'm not ready to sleep yet."

I had the feeling that he was holding something back.

Maybe holding a lot back.

Part of me wanted to call him out on it, but I didn't know if I was ready to deal with the consequences of that.

"Sure," I agreed.

With his magic fading out of my system, I was starting to remember what he'd been feeling.

One thing in particular.

Devotion.

I didn't know what to do about that. On one hand, we were going to be mated for the rest of our lives. We would be together in the next life, too, thanks to the bond we'd created. Some amount of devotion or connection seemed natural, given the bond between us.

But how much of that could he feel before devotion became something more?

How long until the line between that and love grew too fuzzy to tell one side from another?

Damian turned a movie on, but my thoughts were somewhere else altogether. Somewhere far from the action that played on the screen.

Somewhere new.

And somewhere more than a little bit terrifying.

eighteen

BLAIR

DAMIAN FELL ASLEEP after the movie ended, but I stayed up late, staring at the wall holding our blank TV.

His arms were around me, and I felt good.

Too good.

I needed to do something about that... didn't I?

I didn't know.

Easing out of his arms just enough to pull my phone from my pocket, I slipped the device free and did what I always did when I was too overwhelmed to work through things by myself.

ME

Can you talk right now?

AVERY

Yep

Izzy's with me

ME

That's fine

Where are you guys?

Avery was the person I talked to when I needed to figure out how to cope with whatever I was dealing with.

Izzy would keep everything I said a secret, so I didn't mind her hearing too. I just couldn't process it on my own.

AVERY

On the roof

We found the door leading up to it a few weeks ago, and Izzy figured out how to pick the lock

Just take the stairs up past your bedroom door

I stared at the message for a minute before finally shaking my head and slipping out.

Following her instructions, I was on the roof two minutes later.

It was a monstrous, open space that made me stop and look around.

An idea occurred to me, and I pulled my phone out, sending a quick message to the assistants. They wouldn't answer until the next day, but that was fine.

I walked across the massive space until I found Izzy and Avery sitting on a blanket, staring up at the stars. Despite the thin layer of fog that was always present in our city, the sky was beautifully clear.

Avery gave me a quick smile as I sat down next to her, and Izzy tossed out a quiet, "Hey."

We all sat together in silence for a few minutes. My mind was still running through my worries on overdrive, but the fresh air eased my tension just a little.

"Are you sure it's safe to be up here?" I asked them.

There were plenty of dragons who might want to take a siren, and they had wings. One in particular that I knew of.

Plenty of winged monsters who could come after us, too.

"Nope," Izzy said, popping her lips on the *p*. "But some risks are worth taking. Getting out here to look at the stars seems like one of them. I miss being outside."

We had a large patio at our house, and Izzy had decked it out with a ton of furniture. She'd always spent a lot of time out there, hating being cooped up.

"I get that," I said. Though I didn't feel it myself, I knew Izzy well enough that I did understand.

"So, what happened?" Avery asked me, her gaze on the sky.

She wasn't going to judge me, no matter what I said. My sisters and I were on the same page about love being dangerous.

"I felt something new in Damian's emotions tonight," I admitted. "Devotion. I don't know what to think about it."

Izzy whistled.

Avery looked over, studying me for a moment before she looked back up at the sky. "I could've told you he felt that, without drinking his emotions."

"Like hell you could."

"The way he looks at you is intense, Blair. He forced you to be his mate, but he did it because he knew he wasn't going to be able to let you walk away."

"That doesn't make it right," I shot back.

"It doesn't," she agreed. "But it should change the way you see your bond."

"Why? In what way?"

Izzy answered. "Because he wants you to be his mate, Blair. His *real* mate. Anyone with eyes can see that. He could use his strength to control you, but he actively gives you control in almost every situation instead."

My mind went back to the first time I convinced him to drink from me more frequently. To our deal.

If he tried hard enough, he could've forced me to drink from him more instead of giving in. Or he could've let me starve until I couldn't take it anymore.

He struggled to give up control, but he did give it up.

Frequently.

"Do you think he's in love with me?" I asked them, fear creeping into my voice.

"I think you know his emotions well enough to figure that out yourself," Avery said gently.

I ran a hand through my hair. It was tangled, but I didn't care.

There was too much else to worry about.

"What would it change if he was?" Izzy asked. "You're already mates. You already live together. He's not letting you go."

"Love is supposed to be dangerous. You know what happened to our moms," I argued.

"Everything is dangerous. Your bond with Hale has made us safer than we've ever been before," Izzy countered.

"Curtis is still after us."

"There are at least a thousand vampires between us and him. We're fine," she said.

I looked at Avery. "You don't agree, do you?"

She met my gaze. "Izzy's right. Being a siren *is* dangerous. Maybe love is too, but if the options are to let yourself fall for Hale or to risk your safety by walking away, there's an obvious answer."

"He wouldn't let me leave if I tried," I said in frustration.

"Have you been down to the security checkpoint recently? Or the parking garage?" Avery asked.

I blinked. "No."

She stood, offering me her arm. I reluctantly followed her lead and took it.

"I'm going to stay here and soak up the starlight. Enjoy your tour," Izzy said.

Avery and I fell into step together as we headed down the stairs and to the elevator on the floor beneath mine.

"How much is Izzy struggling?" I asked Avery, knowing she was the only one everyone really talked to about that stuff.

"More than she'll admit. She doesn't feel like she fits here. You know how independent she is."

I frowned. "We need to get rid of Curtis, so she can have more freedom."

"Have you talked to Hale about that?"

"No." Something in her expression made me suspicious. "What have you heard?"

"Clem has me spending time with her and the vampires when Zora gets tired of them. A few of them were talking about an argument someone overheard between Hale and a werewolf last week."

My forehead creased. "An argument over the phone?"

"No. I guess he has an old friend who's a wolf, and they met in his office."

The crease deepened.

I remembered him mentioning someone who might be able

to help with the situation, but last he'd told me, he hadn't been able to get in contact with him.

"If they met in our wing of the Manor, Damian trusts him," I said.

"I would assume so. He hasn't mentioned it?"

"No, but we spend most of our time together playing our game," I admitted. "I've been avoiding deep conversations, but I'll ask him. Maybe his solution could pan out."

"Maybe." Avery lifted a shoulder.

We reached the security checkpoint, and I stopped before we walked through.

One of the guards waved at us, and I frowned again when he didn't move to stop us.

"You're not a prisoner here any more than we are," Avery told me. "Watch." She towed me through the security gate and down the hallway. We turned the corner and left, without anyone yelling, calling out behind us, or grabbing us.

We really *were* free.

"We shouldn't go any further," I said, looking around the hallway of the neutral building we'd officially entered. The guy at the reception desk waved at us, and I recognized him from that first night.

Johnny, I think his name was?

He jogged over to us, his eyes bright. "Hey, it's been a while. How are things going?"

"Pretty well," I said, looking over my shoulder and then looking past him, toward the entrance to the wolves' building.

He asked us something about our new rooms, and when I didn't answer, Avery chatted politely with him.

As soon as she got the chance to end the conversation, we slipped back into the hallway.

"I haven't heard from Damian. I'm surprised his guards didn't call him," I whispered, as we walked deeper into the hall.

"Maybe they did."

"He would be here already if he knew I was trying to leave," I said.

"Do you think he'd try to stop you more than the guards did?"

I didn't have to think about the answer. "If I wanted to leave, he would just insist on going with me. But if he thought I was risking my life, he'd drag my ass back to our room."

Avery's lips curved upward. "You could do a lot worse."

"I know."

It was the truth, but it made everything more complicated.

"Let's go see the garage," I said.

She agreed, and off we went.

THIRTY MINUTES LATER, we parted ways at the elevator as she headed to her room and I went to mine.

When I asked for a set of keys, the parking attendant hadn't even hesitated to give me one. It was the middle of the night, and I was the king's mate, yet no one batted an eye at my request to leave.

I was still surprised that I hadn't heard from Damian when I got up to our room.

When I saw his phone on the floor next to the bed, the screen lit up, and I understood. I'd lowered the canopy for him before I left, so he hadn't seen or heard it ringing.

I left it there, lifting the canopy so I could slip into bed with him before I lowered it once again.

His body was deliciously warm beneath mine, and I hesitated for a moment before I made it back to my side of the bed.

Though I settled back down on my pillow just fine, and the cold wasn't horrible, I couldn't help but stare at Damian's peaceful, sleeping face.

My mind kept moving.

Kept returning to that one emotion.

Devotion.

Love.

Whether he realized he felt that for me or not, Damian loved me.

And that was terrifying.

I bit my lip, remembering what my sisters had said about him letting me have control.

Giving me control.

I couldn't stop myself from remembering a conversation he and I had.

Well, two conversations.

The first night, he'd told me his body was free game. That if I was horny, I was free to use him, and he'd wake up to join me.

And another time, when I wanted to put my mouth on him. He told me then that if I wanted that much power over him, I was going to have to catch him off guard.

He had offered me control over him, to a much larger extent than I'd ever given him power over me.

Minus the part where he made me agree to be his mate, that is.

And really, the fact that I was his blood mate made that part unavoidable. He would never have been able to let me go. Considering that I was a siren, leaving me unmarked would've been dangerous for him, too.

He'd made the only reasonable decision he could in his situation.

So, maybe it was time to let my grudge go.

And maybe it was time to take a little more of the power he'd offered me.

With a long breath, I peeled the pillow from between us and set it to the side.

Then, I took its place beside my mate.

My heart beat quickly as I slipped my hand into his boxer-briefs, finding him already hard.

His cock jumped as I wrapped my fingers around him and stroked slowly, once. His hips rocked lightly, and I bit my lip as I released his erection.

His breathing remained even.

I slipped my oversized shirt and bra over my head, tossing them aside. My panties would've been a pain to get off, so I left them on.

Knowing exactly what would drive Damian the craziest, I slipped a leg over his chest, leaving my ass facing him as I lowered my lips toward his cock. All he would see was my backside when he woke up to my mouth on him—and there were few things he loved as much as my ass.

He shifted a little in his sleep as I dragged his boxers down just enough to free his erection.

And though I wasn't the most experienced at blowjobs, I wrapped my hand around the base of his thick erection and wrapped my lips around him.

His hips jerked violently as I took him deep into my mouth, and I heard a gasped, *"Fuck,"* before his hands were gripping my ass.

The curse fit perfectly, because the way he tasted was surreal.

Addicting.

Delicious.

I waited a moment, giving him time to throw me off his lap, just in case he wasn't as sure about being woken up by my mouth as he'd said.

Instead, he spread my ass cheeks and growled.

I bobbed my head, and his hips rocked to meet me. I could tell he was trying not to take what he wanted and thrust deep into my throat, and appreciated it. It would take me more than one blowjob to be ready for that.

I gasped around his cock when he tore my panties to the side and filled me with his fingers roughly.

Shit, that felt good.

He pulled his fingers out and dragged them over my back entrance.

The sensation was *electrifying*.

I lifted my ass, taking him deeper into my mouth, and he snarled out another curse before he pushed a finger into my back entrance.

I cried out around his mouth, earning another growl as he thrust his hips lightly.

I took him deeper, and he swore viciously. I sucked, and he roared, hips jerking and cock throbbing as his release flooded my throat. It was overwhelming, in the very best way.

In one powerful motion, he rolled us over so he was on top of me, his cock still in my mouth. He ripped my panties off entirely and buried his face between my thighs, pushing his finger deeper into my back entrance as I cried out in pleasure.

He worked me hard with his tongue until I shattered once, but he didn't stop teasing my clit until I came again.

Before I knew what he'd done, he sank the tip of one of his fangs into my clit.

His magic canceled out the pain, like always—and all I felt was pleasure.

Hot, *electric* pleasure.

I screamed as I rocked against him, chasing the high of my climax. He released me when it finally started fading, dragging his tongue slowly over me as I healed.

I was squirming again when he licked me for the last time, wiping his scruffy chin on the inside of my thigh to make me shiver.

He turned me around the right way and pulled me into his

arms, holding me tightly. I realized as the wetness between my thighs slid down my ass, that I was laying on my pillow.

The one I usually used as a fence.

"You put me on the pillow on purpose, didn't you?" I mumbled.

"Never," he drawled, sleep in his voice.

"You're kinky in the middle of the night."

"All bets are off if you wake me up with your mouth. Or cunt. I'm still waiting for you to sit on my face."

I fought the urge to bite my lip, my face warm. "You're going to be waiting a while."

"Unless you give me permission to wake *you* up when *I* want you."

I was a goner.

A total goner.

"Alright," I whispered.

His eyes met mine. "Are you sure?"

"Mostly."

His lips curved upward. "I'll give you a chance to turn me down."

"Then it's a definite yes."

He kissed me, and his mouth tasted like my pleasure.

I wasn't sure whether to be disgusted or turned on by that. Considering that I was still a little horny, the second won out.

He closed his eyes, and I shifted against him a little, trying to get his erection into the perfect position.

"You want more?" There was no judgment in his voice, but my stomach tensed a little anyway.

When he opened his eyes, I saw the wicked gleam in them, and my self-consciousness vanished.

"Needy little siren," he all but purred.

I heard fabric rustling, and nearly groaned when I felt the head of his cock at my entrance.

"We both know you love me needy," I breathed, and he grinned as he thrust inside me.

"Unquestionably."

WHEN WE HAD CLIMAXED TOGETHER AGAIN, Damian tossed the pillow to the very far side of the bed and pulled me into his arms.

"You really don't like that thing, do you?" I murmured against his neck.

"I despise it, actually." He kissed my head lightly.

"No more pillow, then."

"Thank fuck for that."

I laughed, and he pulled me closer.

I curled into his arms and let myself consider what it might be like if I let myself look at us as real mates, just for a moment.

And honestly?

I liked the idea so much it hurt.

nineteen

BLAIR

I WAS PLASTERED to Damian's chest with sweat and who knew what else when I eventually woke up.

Despite the discomfort of the sweat, I felt more rested than I'd been in a long time.

Though I wanted to blame that change on feeding from him the night before, I knew it was just having his arms around me like that. The physical contact alone was enough to relax me.

One of his arms was wrapped around my waist, holding me securely against him. His hand was on my back, stroking my skin lightly, and it made me feel so good I wanted to melt. "Good morning, little siren."

His murmur made my lips curve upward just a little.

"Good morning." I didn't lift my head from where it was tucked against him.

"I got a few messages about you trying to leave the Manor while I was sleeping."

Ah.

Right.

"I didn't believe my sisters when they said I wasn't a prisoner. Avery proved it. Your security team didn't try to stop me. The guy in the parking garage gave me keys."

His arm tightened around me. "Of course you're not a prisoner. I just need you to stay safe. With me."

"Are you going to tell them not to let me go next time?"

"No. I'm going to keep my phone closer if there's going to be a next time."

There was no question in his voice, but I didn't want him to think I was going to be sneaking out or anything. "There won't be. If I ever want to leave, I'll let you know."

I felt his grip loosen a little. "Thank you."

"Mmhm. But if I'm going to start telling you things like that, you have to tell me all of the important things too."

"You heard about Porter?"

"Is that the werewolf's name?"

Damian sighed. "Yeah. He's an old friend."

"Why were you meeting with him? And why were you fighting?"

"Porter's family ran the pack in Mistwood for centuries, up until another alpha challenged his father and killed him. Werewolf law required the challenger to let Porter's mother and siblings leave, but he killed them too. Porter wasn't there when all of that happened, but as soon as he heard, he came back to town and tore the new alpha to shreds. Rather than staying to lead the pack like the law indicated he should, he abandoned it. Curtis rose to power instead."

My eyebrows lifted against Damian's skin. "So he's the real alpha?"

"The rightful alpha, yes, but not the real alpha. Curt has hold of the pack's magic. He's in charge in every way, he just didn't fight Porter for the right the way wolves are supposed to."

"Oh. So you called him in to meet with him because..."

"Because if I kill Curtis, it'll start a war. But if Porter kills him, it'll create peace," he said simply. "All of the other leaders know and trust Porter, too. If we can set him up as the pack's alpha, all of us can relax our security here at the Manor and focus on our people like we did before Curt came into power."

"And my sisters would be free."

"They would still be in some danger as long as they're unmated, but yes. My vampires could protect them well enough that you could all slip out into the city from time to time without too much risk."

"So why were you fighting?"

Damian let out an annoyed breath. "He won't come back for free."

"What does he want?"

"You don't want to know."

"I do."

He pulled me up a little higher on his body, so my forehead pressed harder against his neck. "He wants to mate with a siren. He knows what you are, and that you must have a pod. No amount of money could convince him—he wants one of your sisters."

My eyes widened. "Seriously? Why?"

"He has demons, and he's been a lone wolf for a long time. I imagine that his mind has been a dark place since he walked away. Your magic could fix that."

I let out an unsteady breath. "We can't give him one of my sisters."

"I know. I told him that. Hence the fighting."

"But there's no other way to convince him to take over for Curtis?"

"No. He made it clear he wouldn't settle for anything else."

"Maybe one of them will agree to feed from him once a month or something instead. Do you think he'd take that?"

"It's unlikely, but if one of them is willing, I could try."

"I'll talk to them."

He kissed my forehead. "I have meetings to get to. Thanks for last night."

My face warmed at the reminder.

Damn, it had been a good night.

"Mmhm." I kissed his throat the way he was always kissing mine, and he shuddered. "Don't like having my teeth so close to your neck?" I teased.

"It's vulnerable," Damian admitted. "But not unpleasant."

I finally slipped off of him, ducking beneath the edge of the canopy as he pressed the button to lift it. "I'll get my sisters together and come find you after I've talked things through with them."

"Alright."

I walked toward the shower, knowing I needed to rinse the remaining salt and other bodily fluids from my skin before I did anything else. "You're following me?" I asked, when I stepped into the shower and realized he was behind me.

"Someone climbed on my cock in the middle of the night. I need a shower too." His chest met my back as he joined me, reaching past me to turn the water on.

I shivered, tilting my head to the side as he kissed my throat. He took a step beneath the water, moving me with him. His erection was against my lower back, his fingers sliding into my hair and tilting my head further. The water falling over us electrified me, and when his teeth brushed my sensitive skin, it only made me want him more.

"You still want me to bite you every day?" he asked.

"Yes." I didn't hesitate.

"You know that means I'm going to fuck you every day."

"I'm counting on it."

His chuckle was low and rumbly, his hand slipping between my thighs. I sucked in a breath as he stroked my clit slowly. "Put your hands in my hair, little siren."

I buried my fingers in the strands, and he grabbed me by my core. I cried out when he lifted me higher, stepping up against the shower's wall.

Water streamed down my skin as my tits met the cold tiles, and I gasped when he thrust into me roughly.

His teeth cut into my throat, and I was a goner.

The man had me completely and utterly under his control, and I was starting to think I actually liked it.

I KNOCKED on the door to Clementine's room an hour later, my hair wet from the shower but my body relaxed.

Damian and I missed breakfast, but he texted the kitchen to request a large, early lunch, and no one was about to turn the king down.

"You're late," Zora said, pulling the door open and looking me up and down suspiciously. "And calm. Too calm."

"I'm always calm." I slipped past her, joining everyone in Clem's room. My eyes met Avery's, and though I saw the question in her gaze, I didn't reply to it.

She'd want to know if I talked to him about the love thing, and I hadn't. Not because I was afraid, but because... well, it was big.

And just because I could drink it from his emotions didn't mean he wanted to talk about it.

"I'm always calm after I've had morning sex with a gorgeous vampire, too," Clem said with a wink. She was sitting on her bed with Zora. Avery was in the desk chair, and Izzy was on the floor, her knees to her chest and her arms draped over them.

"I've done no such thing." I sat on the edge of the desk, since there was nowhere else to sit. "But if I had, it would've been excellent."

Zora snorted.

Clem laughed.

Izzy and Avery were both watching me. They'd probably realized that if I was making jokes, it was to lighten the mood before I dropped some unfortunate truths.

"I talked to Damian about the wolf he met with," I said. "His name is Porter, and apparently, he's the rightful alpha. He killed the last one, but left afterward. Curtis took over when he was gone."

Four sets of eyebrows lifted.

"Damian has been trying to convince him to take Curt out, because if a vampire does it, it's a declaration of war. Damian can't get involved directly without risking his people, which he won't do."

"And we won't ask him to," Clem said firmly.

She would sooner walk into Curtis's arms herself than let him start a war. Clearly, the woman loved vampires. Maybe even more than I did, and I was mated to one.

"No," I agreed. "He's been talking to Porter, trying to get him to challenge Curtis so he can take over the pack. But Porter found out that he's mated to me and put it together that you all exist."

Izzy's eyes narrowed.

Avery grimaced.

"He's not willing to take any other kind of payment now. He wants one of you as his mate, to help him fight the demons in his mind with your magic."

"Fuck," Izzy said.

Clem ran a hand through her hair. "That's not good."

"He can screw right off," Zora said.

Avery's grimace just deepened.

"If you're willing, I was thinking we could try to offer for one of you to feed from him once a month, or once a week or something. Maybe we could get what we want, and still give him what he wants," I suggested.

"There's no way he'll accept that," Izzy said. "He would have no guarantee that we'll keep up our side of the deal. With Curtis dead, he'd lose any bargaining chip he possessed. He won't take anything except a mate bond."

"Then we'll just stay here," Zora decided. "The vampires can keep us safe, and we like it here. They're cool. We don't need to leave the Manor."

Clem nodded. "It's not worth one of us giving up our freedom for it."

Avery agreed. "I'm not willing to mate with someone just so I can leave."

Everyone looked at Izzy.

Her bottom lip was between her teeth. Usually, she made decisions quickly, and didn't change her mind about them.

We waited.

Her lip popped free, and familiar certainty settled on her face. "I'll do it."

I blinked.

The rest of us did too.

"I can't be trapped here forever," she said. "I'm losing my mind. Hale knows Porter, right? Does he trust him?"

I nodded slowly. "All of the leaders do."

"Then he can't be that bad. I'll mate with him. He'll kill Curtis, and we'll be free again."

"That's insane," Zora protested. "It's great here. We have an amazing pool, and the vampires treat us well. Plus, they're always willing to feed us."

"I'm sorry, but I can't spend my life trapped in this building with vampires," Izzy said firmly. "I don't want to. I won't."

"The wolves are *worse*, not *better*," Clementine argued.

"If he's not going to treat me like shit, I'll figure it out. I just can't stay here forever," Iz repeated.

"It's her choice," Avery said. "If she wants to leave, this is probably her best opportunity to do that. The werewolf alpha will be able to keep her safe, and he'll buy the rest of us a little more security, too."

"You guys deserve not to live in fear of Curtis anymore. We all do," Izzy said, rising to her feet. "Let's go tell Hale."

Zora put her hands out. "You should at least think this through a little longer."

"You know that's not really my style." Izzy flashed her a small grin.

Zora sighed, shaking her head. "You're insane."

"Maybe a little."

Worried about the turn of events, I followed Izzy out of

Clem's room. She slipped her hands into the pockets of her ripped, baggy jeans as the door shut behind us.

"Are you sure about this?" I asked her.

"Do you regret mating with Hale?"

The question made me blink.

"If you could go back in time and refuse, would you do it?" she added.

"No," I admitted. "But all of us would've been at Curtis's mercy if I turned him down."

"And all of us will be trapped here if I don't mate with Porter," Izzy said. "I don't think I could regret choosing freedom."

"What if he's worse than you think?" I asked. "What if you're not attracted to him? Or his past is more haunting than you expect? Or—"

"I can handle whatever I need to," she said firmly. "A little darkness is a small price to pay to save myself from a life of fear. Seeing Curtis dead will make it worth it."

"It's your decision. But I'm kind of with Zora about thinking it through a little more."

"I'll have time to back out if I want to after seeing what he looks like."

She didn't say it, but I knew she wouldn't back out. When Izzy made her mind up about something, she didn't change it.

"At least I won't be the only woman at the kings' meetings anymore," I said.

She smiled. "They'll regret forcing us to be their mates when we steal their thrones."

I laughed.

Something told me Damian would sit me on his throne himself if I asked him to.

twenty
DAMIAN

"I'M HAPPY FOR YOU," Egan said, leaning back in his chair across from my desk. "You've obviously won the woman over, despite the shit that went down when you met."

"I wouldn't say that, but we're getting there."

And I fucking loved where we were.

Blair and Izzy slipped into my office before I could ask him about our newest guards, and he winked at me before he stood up.

"Good luck, Hale."

He greeted them on his way out, and they mirrored the pleasantries.

There were two chairs in front of my desk, and the women each took one.

I looked at Blair, tipping my head toward her desk chair. I didn't want my mate sitting across from me, as if she answered to me the same way everyone else did.

She shook her head, and I fought the urge to tighten my jaw.

The woman drove me mad.

Absolutely, utterly insane.

And I lived for it—but I thought we were past the point of her sitting across from me the way she was.

I leaned back in my chair. "Something tells me I should be concerned when you both come into my office like this."

Izzy folded her arms. "I'm going to mate with Porter."

My eyebrows lifted.

Blair grimaced. "We're hoping you can talk her out of it, Damian."

Her use of my first name eased my irritation at the distance she'd put between us.

"No one's going to talk me out of it," Izzy said bluntly. "I don't want to be trapped inside any longer. I know the wolves have lots of land behind their portion of the Manor, so I'd have more space there. Getting rid of the threat to Clementine and the rest of my sisters is just a bonus. I'm doing it for me, not for them."

I couldn't deny that I liked her answer. She could ensure my mate's safety. Porter had a damn good chance of beating

Curtis. I wouldn't lie to anyone by claiming I was absolutely confident he could win, but given the pack's history, it was likely.

Overall, he was our best chance.

But he wouldn't fight without the promise of a siren to mate with him.

If she was offering that, there was no way I could turn her down. Not from a leadership perspective, when it could promote peace with the wolves. And certainly not from a mate perspective, when I knew Curtis would be giddy at the chance to hurt my female if he ever had the opportunity.

"You're not telling her no," Blair grumbled, though she didn't look surprised.

"I'm trying to think of a way to say yes without making you hate me again."

Blair groaned. "Not you too."

"It's the best option, and we all know it," Izzy said. "He's not cruel, is he?"

"Porter? No. He's distant, though. He probably wouldn't try to bond with his wolves if he were the alpha. Truthfully, I don't know that he would try to bond with his mate any more than he had to, either."

"This just gets even better. Do you have a picture of him?" Izzy checked.

I glanced at Blair. Though she didn't look happy, she didn't look like she despised me the way she had when I all but forced her to agree to be my mate.

That was good.

Probably.

I pulled up a picture of me, Porter, and Bane when we were younger, turning the computer screen around so they could see it.

"At least he's hot," Izzy put in.

"You were all friends?" Blair asked.

"Yes. Power forces you to befriend others with similar strength, to avoid issues," I said.

"What's he like?"

"He used to be the wildest and most rebellious of the three of us. I've only seen him a few times since his family was killed, and he's been very quiet and serious. When I try to spend time with him, he hangs up or goes off the grid."

"So his baggage is heavy," Izzy said, propping her feet up on my desk.

Blair's eyes flicked to me, like she was worried I'd care about her sister's feet, but I didn't give a damn. It was just a desk.

"Very heavy."

"Well, I'm in. How does it work from here?"

"I'll call him back and let him know you're willing. He'll insist on sealing the bond before he challenges Curtis. I'll agree, but ensure you stay with me until the bastard is dead for safety purposes. He'll issue a challenge immediately."

"How long until he comes for me after you call him?" she asked.

"He won't want to give you time to change your mind, so I imagine he'll be here within a few hours. He lives outside the city, so that's as fast as he can make it."

She nodded. "When do you want to do it?"

"That's entirely your call, Izzy," I said.

"You should give it a few days," Blair put in, her gaze fixed on her sister. "So you have time to think it through. If he's not going to let you change your mind, you need to make sure you're positive."

Izzy flashed her a small smile. "I've been trying to come up with a way to leave that doesn't risk my life since we got here, Blair. I'm not going to change my mind." She looked at me. "Call him. I want to see how he responds."

"You can't give orders to a king," Blair warned. "And *don't* deny that you're the king, Damian." She shot me a warning look that had me lifting my hands in surrender.

"Technically, I'm about to become a queen. So we're equals," Izzy pointed out.

I chuckled.

Blair sighed, sitting back in her chair. "You're going to make that wolf regret his decision, aren't you?"

"Probably," Izzy's voice was upbeat, as if she liked the idea.

I turned my computer back around and hit the button to start a video call.

The women slipped out of their chairs and came around my desk. Though they stayed far enough to the side that they weren't in the video, they could see the screen.

Porter picked up at the last second.

"If you're not calling to tell me you convinced one of your mate's sisters to be mine, I'm hanging up," he said flatly.

"My mate still doesn't have any sisters," I lied smoothly.

He would know it was a lie, but acknowledging the truth would give him leverage. And power. Which I wasn't going to allow. If Izzy wanted to let him meet her sisters, that was a decision she would make for herself.

"Fuck off."

Before he could end the call, I said quickly, "But another siren has come to me requesting protection. She's agreed to mate with you in exchange for the same."

Porter's eyes narrowed slightly. "She's willing?"

"Yes. And hungry."

"I'll be there before the sun goes down."

"You'll challenge Curtis before she'll leave with you, of course."

"I'll send the message to set up the fight on my way to the city. It'll happen tonight. Let the other leaders know."

With that, Porter hung up.

"Well, that told me absolutely nothing about him," Izzy grumbled. "He didn't even bat an eye when you said I was going to mate with him."

"He was calm the whole time. He doesn't seem to have much of a temper, at least," Blair offered.

"He's subdued his personality to the extent that I doubt you'll see much emotion from him," I agreed. "You'll be safe."

Izzy's expression said something along the lines of, *"fuck being safe"*.

"I'm going to go pack my stuff. Thank you," she said, her gratitude pointed to me. It seemed genuine.

She closed the door behind herself, leaving me alone with my female.

"So," Blair said, leaning her hip against my desk.

"So," I repeated, turning my chair so I could study her.

"Should I be worried about Izzy?" she asked.

"No. Porter will respect her, when he's with her."

"You don't think he'll be with her often?"

"I think he wants her magic to try to find some part of himself that disappeared when he lost his family. And until he does—*if* he does—he's going to put as much distance between them as he can."

Blair grimaced. "If she realizes he's doing that, she's going to push back."

"Then maybe she'll be able to break him out of his funk."

"Or maybe he'll break her heart."

I lifted a shoulder. "Either way, it's their decision to make."

"I guess. I just don't like knowing she could end up hurting and there's nothing I can do to prevent it. But she made her choice."

"Just as you made yours, when you walked in here and sat *across* from me, like you aren't *my* queen." I stood, stepping up to her so our chests nearly brushed.

"I wasn't going to sit across from my sister like I was in charge," she tossed back. "You think I'm the queen, but no one else does."

"*Everyone* else does."

"That's a lie, and you know it."

I took a step closer, pressing her front to mine as I leaned over and hit a button on the phone on my desk. It rang once before a male voice answered.

"Hello?"

"Hi, Charlie. It's Hale. My queen requested peppermint brownies with dinner tonight." Our gazes were locked as I spoke.

"I'll make it happen," Charlie promised, not missing a beat. "Tell Blair to send me her preferences in the future. We're happy to adjust our menu for her."

"I will. Thank you."

"Of course." He ended the call, and neither of us looked away.

"You never call yourself the king," she finally said. "You don't even let anyone else call you that."

"It's unnecessary. But you will *always* be known as the queen."

"That's unnecessary too."

"Not to me."

I lifted a hand to her face, and she closed her eyes as I cupped her cheek. Tilting her head, I lowered my lips to her ear. "This is our office. The next time you come in here with anyone, you sit in your chair or on my lap."

"What if I want *your* chair?"

I chuckled. "Then I perch on the armrest, making it clear who you belong to."

"The mark on my throat does a pretty good job of that, don't you think?"

"I do." I tilted her head further, so I could drag the tip of my tongue slowly over the sensitive mark. She shivered, and I sucked lightly on her skin.

One of her fists clenched in my shirt. She'd wrinkle it, but I liked walking around with evidence of the way my female had grabbed me.

The scent of her arousal made my erection thicker, and I lifted her onto the edge of my desk. She sucked in a breath as I pressed the base of my palm against her core.

"I'm supposed to be meeting Kara and Lou for my last injection right now," she breathed.

"I haven't tasted you yet today." I kneeled between her thighs.

She bit her lip.

"You're the one who wanted me addicted, woman. No taking it back now." I peeled her pants down her thighs, tossing them across the office.

"Alright, make it quick."

I lifted my gaze to hers, finding her cheeks pink and her eyes bright. "You don't want it quick."

"Yes I do."

I leaned in and dragged my tongue around her clit slowly. She moaned so loudly, my assistants could probably hear it down the hall. I repeated the motion as her hips moved, her hands burying in my hair as she pulled the strands harder.

"Faster," she panted, and I slowed down even more. "Fuck you."

"You will, little siren."

She kicked my side halfheartedly, and I dragged the tip of my fang over her clit, making her gasp. "Damian!"

I resumed my slow tease, making her moan and arch as I worked her body.

"I need you," she said, her voice growing desperate.

I filled her with two of my fingers as I finally picked up the pace like she wanted, and she came hard around them, her channel tightening with her pleasure in that way I fucking lived for.

My computer started playing the tune that meant someone was video calling me, and I growled against her core. It was probably my next financial meeting—but they could wait.

Blair's face was flushed as she pushed me toward my chair. "You have meetings."

"They'll wait."

I wasn't going to stop before I'd had my mate again, that was for damn sure.

"No, Damian." Her insistence surprised me. She pushed me toward my chair, slipping off the desk and tucking herself beneath it.

My cock nearly broke through my zipper when I realized what she was saying.

What she was doing.

Some part of me couldn't stand the idea of letting her control me that way while I was on a video call.

But there was a challenge in her eyes—and ultimately, I trusted her.

And wanted her.

I wiped my face on my sleeve and sat down in my chair, wheeling it up to my desk as I hit the button to answer the call.

My greeting was automatic, though every cell in my body was focused on the woman beneath my desk.

She unbuttoned my jeans, and I gripped the armrests on my chair as she undid the zipper.

My jaw clenched as I fought to stop myself from reacting when she wrapped those pretty little lips around my cock.

My female was in no hurry, having her way with me slowly throughout the meeting.

My responses were clipped as I tried to end the call quickly, but it droned on as she licked me.

Sucked me.

Teased me.

Took me deep enough into her throat to make me choke back a snarl.

Fed from me, just to make me lose my mind even further.

But she pulled away every time I got close to coming down her throat.

When the meeting finally ended, I snarled loudly, hauling her sexy little ass out from beneath my desk and dropping her on the edge as I slammed into her, making her cry out as I took her.

I bit her as I pumped my release into her tight channel, making her come with me once, then again, until we were both panting as we came down from the high.

"You drive me insane," I growled into her hair.

She laughed breathlessly. "You love it."

"So much it hurts."

I kissed her hard, tasting myself on her tongue the way she probably tasted herself on mine.

"How many of those pointless financial meetings do you sit through every day?" she asked.

"Too many."

"Maybe you should tell them to email you a summary, and spend the time on something else instead. You always have a million things to do."

"Maybe I should." I kissed her again, slower.

"I really do have to go," she said against my mouth. "I'll meet you for our early lunch afterward, though?"

"Alright. Let me know if you want me to join you for the injection."

She rolled her eyes. "I think I can handle it."

I knew she could—but I didn't want her to have to.

She made sure her clothes were on right, then slipped out of our office with a wink over her shoulder.

I was so fucking in love with her.

twenty-one

BLAIR

I WAS STILL red-faced and out of breath when I finally made it to the hospital portion of Vamp Manor.

"I know I'm insanely late, I'm sorry," I apologized as I made it through the door. Lou and Kara were talking, neither of them looking annoyed that I was more than an hour late. "I would say it was Damian's fault, but it was mine too, so let's just leave it at an apology," I said, dropping into the chair I always took during my injections.

Lou's nose wrinkled. "You smell like sex."

"Give us all the details," Kara ordered.

Lou made a gagging face. "Don't even think about it."

I wouldn't have given Kara the details even if Lou wasn't there, so I just shook my head.

Kara grabbed the tiny injection tube. "Did you talk him into feeding every day yet?"

"Yeah, he finally came around yesterday. Definitely seems to be doing good today," I said, my face flushing further.

Part of me couldn't believe I'd gone beneath his desk and taken him in my mouth like that, but the other part of me couldn't stop thinking about how much fun I'd had.

And wanting to do it again.

"You're a hero," Kara said, a knowing look on her face.

"Thank you," Lou said, her expression grateful. "I'm sure he makes it good for you—but thank you for taking care of him. He needed that desperately."

"He takes care of me too," I admitted. "We've never really acknowledged being mates in the real way, but I think we might be moving toward that. I'm not sure. I know his feelings for me are growing, but he hasn't said anything about it. And I'm just... it's a lot."

"What do you mean, in a real way?" Kara asked. Her voice was curious.

My face flushed warmer. "He forced me to mate with him, remember? I'm over it now, I know it was his best option. But when we sealed the bond, we agreed that nothing was going to change. We were going to keep hating each other, and feed from each other just because the bond demanded it. We never talked about being anything more than that."

"You haven't hated each other for a long time now," Lou pointed out.

"Longer than I want to admit."

"Then what's not real about your bond?" Kara asked me.

"I don't know. We had rules against the normal mate stuff, like holding hands and snuggling and having vulnerable conversations. We snuggled for the first time last night."

"That's ridiculous," Kara grumbled.

I sighed. "It seemed like a good way to stop myself from developing feelings for him at the time."

"And what about now?" Lou asked.

"I don't know."

It was the truth.

I'd just kneeled beneath his desk and given him a blowjob during a boring financial meeting—which was absolutely insane—but I still didn't know if I could tell him that I loved him.

Or if he was sure enough about his emotions to admit that he loved me too.

What if I opened up to him, and he told me he didn't feel the same way?

Or what if he wanted me to keep hating him?

There were a million things that could go wrong if I admitted the truth, and so very few ways it could go right.

I needed to be sure before I opened up, didn't I?

"How does he feel about you?" Kara asked, finally injecting me. "You have to know, don't you?"

I nodded. "He loves me. But some emotions are buried deep. I don't know if *he* knows that he loves me. If I tell him I think I feel the same way, and he hasn't realized his feelings yet, it could ruin everything. It's a risk. And I don't usually take risks."

I wasn't like Izzy—I couldn't mate with a stranger just to get out of Vamp Manor. I'd done it because there was no other way to protect myself and my sisters. And even though I knew now that Damian wouldn't have really given us to Curtis, I hadn't known that at the time.

If I had, I might've refused him.

And who knew what would've happened from there.

"He never hated you," Lou said. "He was just trying to cope with the mate bond, and made a mess of it. I tore into him for forcing you to bond with him."

"I'm starting to believe that." I ran a hand through the top of my hair, making a mess of the golden waves. Damian had already done the same, so it wasn't like they could get much worse. "I think I just need more time to work through my feelings."

"He's your mate, honey. You've got all the time in the world." Kara put a Band-Aid over the injection site, even though we both knew it was unnecessary. "You're all set."

"Thank you." I gave her a quick hug, and hugged Lou too before heading out to meet Damian.

After lunch, I was meeting up with my sisters.

We'd help Izzy pack... and then we'd go for a swim, just in case it was a while before we saw her again. We could hope like hell that her mate wouldn't keep her from us, but with how much she wanted to get away, I was worried about how often we'd see her.

She was insane for agreeing to seal a bond with Porter.

But, like Damian said, it was her decision to make. And I had to respect that, even if I wanted to lock her in a room and force her to see how crazy she was.

HOURS LATER, a large rock came sailing down to the bottom of the pool. I recognized it as one we'd rescued from our house—one of the only things Curtis's guys hadn't destroyed, because they didn't realize the rocks held meaning for us.

I caught Clementine's eye, gesturing toward the surface, and she grabbed Izzy's shoulder. All of us swam upward and slipped out of the pool.

Damian was waiting beside the water, his hands in his pockets and his sleeves rolled up his forearms like usual.

My gaze lingered on his arms.

Damn, he was pretty.

"Porter's waiting in my office," he said. Though the words were for Izzy, his gaze lingered on me.

"Guess it's time to meet the pretty bastard," Izzy said, her voice far from upbeat. She didn't usually do upbeat, though.

Sarcasm definitely, but optimism? Not typically. She wasn't pessimistic, but she was very much a realist.

Damian pulled his button-up over his head and tugged it over mine. I rolled my eyes at him, but didn't argue when he buttoned it up to my chin.

Zora snorted.

Clem whispered, "At least he didn't throw her over his shoulder and carry her up to his room to have his way with her again."

"Eventually, you will both know what it means to be mated to a big, possessive bastard," I warned.

"There are perks," Damian tossed out.

"Big perks," I admitted, albeit a little reluctantly.

"Big, *hard* perks," he drawled.

All of us busted up laughing, though Izzy only managed a small smile.

She'd learn about those particular perks pretty soon. And I'd heard enough about how much she enjoyed sex to be positive she wouldn't regret the mate bond for that reason, even if there was regret on other fronts.

Damian took my hand, lacing his fingers through mine as we headed off.

Our walk to the elevator and then down the hallway to Damian's office was short, but the mood grew much more serious as we went. Worry made my abdomen tight.

I worried about Izzy taking a mate... but more than that, I worried about the worst outcome of the coming hours.

Porter could *lose* after he challenged Curtis.

Curtis could be even more set in his ego and even more of a dictator afterward.

He could want us even more for conspiring against him.

And that would be really, really bad.

We probably should've hidden the rest of my unmated sisters, but one look at the three of them told me they were going to meet Izzy's mate, consequences be damned.

Maybe we could claim they were sirens in need of help too, if we had to.

Porter was waiting outside Damian's office. He was bigger than he'd seemed on the video call—maybe even as big as Damian. He had tan skin and wild, reddish-brown hair that was shaved on the sides but longish on the top.

When he asked Izzy for a minute alone, she agreed, and slipped inside with him.

We heard a thud against the door a moment later.

My sisters and I exchanged looks of surprise.

"Damn, they didn't waste any time," Zora whistled.

"He's so hot, I'd screw him too if he asked," Clementine whispered conspiratorially.

"Don't let Izzy hear you say that after he's her mate," Avery warned.

All three of them looked at me, and I had a feeling similar things had been said about Damian.

My hand tightened on his, and he squeezed it lightly.

He was mine.

That was what mattered.

And my sisters could be horny, but none of them would ever dream of screwing a mated man. Mated pairs were solidly off-limits.

A few minutes after that, the couple finally stepped back out. Their faces were red and they were breathing faster than usual.

The black marks around their throats drew my attention immediately. They were pretty, swirling bands that I knew Izzy would love even without asking.

From there, we headed down the hallway.

And to the neutral territory.

Zora, Clementine, and Avery all hugged Izzy and whispered, "Good luck," before staying in the vampire wing of the Manor.

We met a massive group of vamp guards in the hallway, led by Egan, and Porter growled an order to Izzy before he strode away without us.

All of us couldn't arrive together.

Not if we didn't want everyone to think we'd teamed up to work against Curtis—and we didn't—so, we had to stay separated.

twenty-two

BLAIR

IZZY WAS SURROUNDED COMPLETELY by huge vampires as Damian pulled me to the front of the group with him. Though he looked calm and collected, his grip on my hand was iron, and he pulled out a length of rope.

"You're not actually going to tie me to you, right?" I whispered.

"I am. If one of these wolves tries to grab you, they're going to be in for a surprise." He slid the rope through one of my belt loops, then one of his, and tied a complex knot.

I sighed, but didn't argue.

If a wolf tried to grab me, I was going to be glad for his paranoia.

There were wolves *everywhere* when we reached the hallway that led into the neutral territory.

Wolves in lines.

Wolves in crowds.

Wolves whispering excitedly.

Wolves wrestling and pummeling each other off to the side of the room.

I imagined being mated to one of them, surrounded by the furry beasts constantly, and shuddered.

Yeah, I liked vampires. Give me fangs and bloodlust, and I was golden.

Then again, there was only one set of fangs I wanted near me.

I bit my lip, glancing sideways at Damian as we stepped toward the mass of werewolves.

"Move," he said to them. His voice was calm, but he stopped and waited for them to obey.

There was something in his tone that warned them not to ignore him.

One of them glanced over, and his face went white when he saw us. Whispers and yelps rolled through the hallway as the crowd parted immediately.

"It shouldn't turn me on that they're so afraid of you," I murmured to Damian, as we resumed walking and made our way down the hall.

"Why not?" He lifted an eyebrow at me, and though he didn't smile, I saw the humor in his eyes.

We made our way through multiple hallways before we finally stepped into what had to have been the largest room I'd ever seen.

My eyes met Curtis's partway across the room—and he looked furious.

"Don't let him see you flinch," Damian said, slowly lifting our intertwined hands so he could kiss the back of my palm.

My gaze left Curt's for a moment, and when I looked back at the werewolf, I saw the fury in his face and movements.

He'd been watching us. That was why Damian kissed my hand.

"Is riling him up really a good idea?" I asked.

"The more furious he is, the more erratic his movements will be, and Porter is anything but erratic in his current condition."

"He didn't seem all that calm and collected in the hallway."

"You'll see. He won't lose." Damian sounded more sure of that than I felt, so I nodded.

A simple metal fence had been set up in the center of the monstrous room, creating a cage of sorts that separated Porter and Curtis from the rest of us. There was a guy standing between them with a microphone in his hand, but he was covering the top as he yelled something to someone behind him.

Porter didn't look in our direction when we found our place just outside the cage, stopping between Bane and Talon.

Our group of vampires was right behind us, with Izzy tucked probably uncomfortably between them.

Bleachers rose around the room, but I tried to ignore the insane noise of the pack of werewolves throughout it.

"Did you arrange this?" Bane called out, looking at me and Damian.

"We would never even consider that," Damian lied, his lips curving upward wickedly.

Bane laughed, and when I looked to my other side, Talon was grinning too.

None of them would be disappointed when Curtis was gone.

...assuming Porter didn't lose.

"Is Kai in the fae realm right now?" Damian asked.

"Yep. He's going to be annoyed he missed this," Bane yelled back.

A few more minutes passed as wolves poured into the room.

"This is the ballroom," Damian said into my ear. "I throw a party here with all the other leaders every year, masquerade-style."

I lifted my face toward his, and he ducked so I could speak into his ear. "If that's your way of inviting me, I'm going to have to pass."

He grinned. "It wasn't an invitation. You're going with me if I have to drag your ass there myself."

I laughed, and he kissed my cheek playfully.

The announcer cleared his throat, and the loud noise carried through the room.

Damian pulled me closer, tucking me between him and the cage.

The announcer's voice boomed when he called into the microphone, "Everyone, shut up!"

The words were far from elegant, but they got the job done as the entire room quieted over the next handful of minutes.

"Let's not waste time," the guy barked. "We're here for a challenge!"

The crowd roared so loudly, I resisted the urge to cover my ears.

Damian chuckled when I winced, his chest rumbling against my back. "Glad I'm not a wolf?" His voice was playful, but he was right.

Very right.

I belonged with the vampires.

I suppose that was what fate was trying to tell me when it made me his blood mate. On second thought, maybe I should've realized it sooner.

"Challenging our beloved alpha, we have Porter Jenkins, the heir to the throne who left us behind two centuries ago," the announcer added.

The crowd roared louder.

I wasn't sure if they were out for Porter's blood, or if they wanted him to win.

Maybe some of both.

"As you know, this is a fight to the death. Last one alive takes the pack. Are we ready?"

More deafening cries flooded the room.

My fingers wrapped around the bars separating us from the wolves as the announcer finally said, "GO!"

The fight began so fast, I jerked backward a little.

I'd been trained as a kid, but was clearly not prepared for a real fight between two of the strongest men alive.

Their fur tore through their skin as they lunged for each other's throats, shifting into their massive wolf forms. Porter's fur was the same reddish-brown color as his hair, and Curt's was blond, so it was easy to tell them apart.

Porter rolled at the last minute, raking his claws through Curtis's belly as Curt sliced through his back.

They landed on the tile and circled each other slowly.

My heart pounded as they sized each other up.

Curtis snapped his teeth toward Porter's throat.

Porter went for Curt's leg, and I heard the crack as he broke the bone.

Curtis used the moment to tear into Porter's shoulder, and

though Porter rolled to the side, he couldn't avoid the deep gash.

Both of them bled as they circled each other again, a little more warily.

Though Curtis limped a little, Porter's shoulder didn't look good at all.

My body was so tense, I could barely breathe.

If Curtis won, we were screwed.

And Izzy...

Holy shit.

Izzy would have a mate bond with a dead man.

She'd be alone, for life.

I wanted to look back at her, to see how she was doing, but didn't let myself look away from the fight. I couldn't miss anything. Not when everything was on the line.

Curtis lunged again, and Porter dodged, tearing into his flank.

When Curtis went for his throat, clearly getting angry, Porter shifted back to his skin and rolled. He took Curtis's wolf down with an iron, human arm around his throat.

As one, the crowd seemed to take a breath.

Curtis snarled, his arms and legs flailing violently as he shifted back too. He grabbed Porter's hair and arms, but Porter seemed to have complete control.

Curt's movements grew weaker, and Porter finally said something into his ear.

Curtis howled—but a moment in, a snapping noise reverberated through the air, and the beastly sound cut off abruptly.

Gasps echoed around us.

Damian let out a relieved breath against my ear.

And then, in an instant, the crowd was roaring.

Porter shoved Curtis's body to the side and stood up, his clothes torn in the shift and abandoned on the tile floor somewhere behind him.

The crowd was screaming for him, making my ears ring with the noise, but his gaze was fixed on me and Damian.

I glanced behind us, at the vampires who had parted to reveal my sister, and realized it wasn't us he was staring at.

He crossed the distance between us and climbed over the fence, dropping to the ground like it was nothing before he strode past us and grabbed Izzy.

She looked taken aback as he lifted her fist toward the ceiling, roaring his victory as his voice joined everyone else's.

The crowd grew deafening, but my gaze was fixed on my sister as her new mate pumped her fist twice—then sank his teeth into her shoulder.

My lips parted as shock filled her expression.

He released Izzy as fast as he'd bitten her, then tossed her over his shoulder and strode out of the room.

The wolves parted for him without hesitation or command, their cheers still filling the room after he was gone.

They started flooding out, but we stayed where we were.

There was no way we were breaking through the wave of wolves without a fight, and no need to start one.

The noise subsided over the next few minutes as the excitement faded and the crowd finally started to thin out.

Damian's hands were still on my hips. "He bit her in front of the crowd," I said, still almost as shocked as Izzy had been. It had surprised me when Damian bit me in front of his people, but he was a *vampire*, so I at least knew it was a possibility.

My sisters and I didn't know enough about the other kinds of magical beings to consider that wolf shifters might bite their mates too.

"Wolves do that. The public claiming thing is big for them," he said, his lips brushing my ear.

"She's going to be pissed at him."

"It only gets worse from there, so something tells me she's going to be pissed at him often."

"Almost like I am at you?" I nudged his abdomen with my elbow, a little playfully.

"Nah, you only pretend to be angry at me these days to get me hard."

"Oh, do I?"

"Yup." He kissed me, pulling me against him so I could feel his erection. "And it works."

I laughed, and he kissed me again, a little longer.

"If that was one of her sisters, I'm going to kill you," Talon grumbled, smacking Damian on the shoulder good-naturedly. "I still need a siren."

"I have no idea what you're talking about," Damian said with a shrug. "But if you need the rest of us to help, you know we've got your back."

"It's not something you bastards can help with. It has to be a siren. An unmated one."

"Well, if we had any unmated sirens—which we still don't —we wouldn't just *give them out*, remember? They would be people, with feelings. And a lack of desire to be handed to a large, terrifying dragon shifter," I said.

Talon cracked a reluctant grin. "I'll take the compliment, at least."

"Don't go smiling at my female," Damian chided, though his expression told me he knew we weren't flirting.

The four of us made our way through the rest of the crowd when there was enough space to get out.

"We'll have to call a meeting in a few days, after Porter has some time to settle things with the pack," Damian said as we went.

The other guys agreed, and after trading *goodbyes*, we headed back to our wing of the Manor with our vampy entourage.

Damian captured my hand, slipping his fingers between mine. Something about it felt ridiculously right.

"I hope Izzy's okay," I said, and he squeezed my hand.

"Porter won't hurt her."

I smiled. "I'm more worried that *she'll* hurt *him*. But she needs people more than she realizes."

"One thing the wolves aren't lacking is people. And physical contact."

I laughed. "They're going to drive her crazy. But maybe it'll be good for her."

"Here's hoping."

Damian pulled me closer as Egan and the rest of our guards headed off in their own directions. My sisters were waiting just beyond the security gate, and descended immediately.

After I explained—in bloody, gruesome detail—everything that happened, they were satisfied.

A little sad, and just as shocked as I'd been about Izzy being bitten by her arranged mate in front of his new pack, but satisfied.

We all headed to the dining room, but Damian and I hung at the back of the crowd.

"I never taught you about your second job," he remarked.

"No, you didn't."

"What do you say we sneak off to our room and bribe one of the kitchen workers to bring us something to eat? I can teach you, or we can watch a movie..." he trailed off, flashing me a grin.

"Hey, you guys are coming to the pool movie night, right?" Zora called over her shoulder.

"I forgot that was tonight," I admitted.

"We can do dinner and the pool," Damian said easily.

He was clearly backing down from what he wanted, to keep the peace. And not to keep the peace with my sisters—to keep the peace with *me*.

But we were mates.

Despite all of my very pointed intentions, real mates. Not just fuck buddies.

And if I'd been the one who didn't want to socialize that night, Damian would've taken my side without question.

It was time for me to start doing the same.

"We're going to stay in and do some work tonight," I called back.

"Is that the code word for sex now?" Clementine teased. It was a little half-hearted, but I knew she was just sad about Izzy leaving. Though I didn't want to leave her to deal with that alone, she had Avery and Zora. Damian only had me.

And though he wasn't struggling with Izzy's departure, he still deserved to have someone there for him.

Besides all of that...

Well, I wanted to hang out with him.

I wanted to spend time with him.

And we needed to have a conversation about the serious things I'd been avoiding talking about.

So yeah, it was a "work" night.

"I'll admit to nothing. Have fun at dinner!" I yelled to them, as they disappeared around the corner.

Damian led me down the hallway that would take us to our elevator, and we slipped inside together.

"You didn't want to hang out with your sisters?" he asked, pulling my chest to his as he leaned up against the elevator's back wall.

"I wanted to hang out with you," I said simply.

His immediate reaction was surprise—and then a slow grin that stretched across his face, lighting up his eyes in a way that told me I'd made the right choice.

He kissed me slowly, and sweetly.

The elevator dinged too soon, and he released my mouth long enough to call out, "Wait for the next one."

Laughter broke out behind me, but when Damian recaptured my mouth, I ignored it.

Some things were just that good.

twenty-three

BLAIR

DAMIAN SENT a message asking for food as we headed into our room.

"I feel disgusting after being there during the fight, so I think I'm going to shower," I said, releasing his hand and heading for the bathroom.

"I'll join you." He tossed his phone onto the bed and followed me.

"Is this a thing we do now?" I teased, slipping my shirt over my head.

"I hope so." He skimmed his hands over the bare curve of my waist before finding the buckle on the back of my bra and unhooking it. The fabric fell away, and he tugged it down my arms, baring me further.

My eyes closed as his hands moved over my breasts, teasing my nipples.

His lips brushed the side of my throat lightly.

My stomach tightened as thoughts about my realizations earlier came to mind.

My feelings.

His emotions.

All the uncomfortable things I didn't want to discuss, but needed to.

Letting out a soft breath, I opened my eyes. "Hey, Damian?"

"Mmhm?" His eyes were on his hands, on my breasts.

"I think we should talk tonight, instead of screwing."

He blinked, then met my gaze. "Talk about what?"

Some inner part of me cringed, but I forced myself to say the word. "Us."

His eyebrows lifted. "Should I be worried?"

"I don't think so."

He dipped his head. "Then we'll talk. But I'm still going to play with your nipples."

A quick laugh escaped me, and his lips curved upward.

We finished stripping, and stepped into the shower together. His hands were on my body almost the entire time we were beneath the water, touching me and teasing me while I washed. Knowing he wasn't trying to turn me on, but just wanted to feel my skin, did strange things to my stomach.

By the time we stepped out, I was even more nervous than earlier.

What if he wasn't ready to acknowledge his emotions?

What if he didn't even realize he felt them?

What if he just wanted our relationship to revolve around sex, and I screwed everything up?

Shit, maybe I'd made the wrong choice.

I reached for one of my oversized sleep shirts, but he grabbed one of his t-shirts off a hanger and tugged it over my head before I got the chance.

"No panties allowed," he said, pulling my hair out from beneath the hem of the shirt.

"Maybe we should just have sex after all, and talk another time?" I suggested.

He finished freeing my hair and grabbed a pair of his underwear. "No. We're not avoiding the conversation if there's something you want to talk about."

I sighed, but didn't argue.

We did need to talk, despite my fear.

He stepped into his boxer-briefs, then captured my hand and towed my reluctant ass to the bed. Rather than sitting in our usual places, he took a seat on the edge of the mattress, and pulled me onto his lap.

His hands caught my hips, and mine landed on his shoulders. "Alright, little siren. What do we need to discuss about us?"

I hesitated.

He stroked my hips lightly, despite the fabric separating him from my skin. The man was clearly not in any kind of a hurry.

I wrestled with my thoughts for another minute before I finally said, "It feels like you think of us as real mates when I drink from you."

He blinked, his hands going still for a moment.

"I'm not saying that's a bad thing," I added hastily. "We just haven't talked about what it means. And I know you might not have realized what you're feeling, because sometimes sirens find emotions that are buried so deep, but—"

"I've never thought of us as anything other than real mates, little siren." He finally resumed stroking my hips, his steady gaze meeting mine.

"Oh," I said, my heart beating hard.

"Oh," he agreed, his lips curving upward. "Do you want to tell me how you think of us?"

"Not particularly."

His lips curved further. "Can I finally tell you how I feel about you, then?"

"Yes."

He released my hips and cupped my face lightly. Gently. Carefully. "I love you, Blair. Deeply. Intensely. In ways I never expected I could when you kissed me in that night-club. I wasn't looking for a mate—but now that I have you, I would do anything and everything to keep you."

"Even build a massive pool and piss off all of your vampires by refusing to build a golf course?"

His lips stretched in a grin. "Even that."

"I found a better place for the mini-golf course. I've been texting our assistants about it. The roof will be perfect for it."

He pulled me closer to his chest. "I don't give a damn about the mini-golf course. Build it if you want. Don't if you don't want to. But right now, we're talking about us."

I nodded, emotion flooding my throat. "I didn't want to fall in love with you."

"I'm aware."

"Love is dangerous," I added, my voice growing softer. "I've seen the way it hurt the people I loved most. My mom warned me not to let myself fall for anyone, over, and over."

Damian nodded.

He knew that, too.

"But loving you doesn't feel like putting myself in danger. It feels... safe. Somehow, in all the fighting and craziness of being bonded to you, you've managed to make me trust you with my heart. I don't know how, or why. And most of me is absolutely terrified—but I do. I trust you. I want you. I love you."

Emotion burned in those gorgeous blue eyes, and he kissed me.

Something about the position brought me back to that night in the club.

The way he'd made me feel at ease.

The way he'd solved my hunger without pressuring me for more.

And for the first time since I'd met him in the Manor, I let myself admit the truth:

He was always the same with me as he had been in the club that night.

Playful. Protective. Charming. Fun.

Sometimes, protecting me meant pressuring me into forming a mate bond with him.

And Damian was the vampire king, but more importantly, he was mine. Forever. The bond made that a certainty.

He released my mouth with one last lingering kiss and finally tucked me against his side, settling on the mattress.

"Why did you stop?" I asked. I enjoyed the snuggling, but I thought he was going to have his way with me.

"I was told we were talking tonight, not screwing."

"We already talked," I pointed out.

"There are at least a hundred other things to talk about if you're finally agreeing to be real mates."

"Like..."

"Like kids. How much responsibility you want when it comes to the Manor. Whether you want to be involved in every communication with the other leaders or want me to handle it. How involved we want to be in public relations with the other wings of the Manor. If—"

I sighed. "Maybe we shouldn't be real mates after all."

He laughed, pulling me closer. "There's no getting free now, little siren. You love me too much." His words were playful, but he was right.

"I know. Alright, let's figure everything out—and then, we'll screw."

"Agreed."

He grabbed the tablet I'd left on one of our nightstands and opened it up to the notes section, making a list of the first handful of discussion topics.

"Kids?" he asked me.

"We can rediscuss that in like five years," I said bluntly. "Right now, it's an immediate no. I'm not bringing more sirens into this world while my sisters still have to hide among the vampires."

Damian agreed. "Alright, next topic."

We moved down the list, with a pause to eat dinner in bed again. The further we went, the more I realized that he didn't particularly care about most of the questions. He just wanted to figure out how *I* felt.

"You know you're allowed to care about this stuff," I told him, gesturing to the list. "If you passionately want me to take on a certain role, I can handle it."

"Right now, the only thing I want passionately is your body wrapped around mine every day. Twice a day." He considered it, then corrected, "*Three* times a day."

I laughed.

We had a lot of sex, but usually not that much. And we both knew he was joking, but that just made it more fun.

"And a bathing suit. For the love of magic, a bathing suit," he added.

"I already agreed not to swim in the nude anymore," I teased.

"Unless we're alone."

"Then, all bets are off."

He kissed me lightly. "Now, back to the list."

I STARTED DRIFTING off as we neared the end of the topics he'd written out. I was sure we would come up with more—there was plenty we hadn't discussed—but we'd covered a lot.

Even a few that Damian *did* care about.

Considering the way he let me make the decisions for most of them, I had no problem agreeing that if one of us had to meet with a clan outside of Mistwood, we would go together.

Or that we would make financial decisions together.

Or that we would combine our bank accounts and actually become a team, the way a mated pair was supposed to. That one was a little harder to accept than the previous two, but when he explained his reasoning, I understood.

I mumbled my answers to a few of the final questions before I actually fell asleep while he wrote them down.

I COULDN'T HAVE SAID how long I was asleep—it could've been a few minutes, or a few hours—but the slow drag of something warm and silky against my clit made me suck in a breath. My hips arched, and I wrestled my eyelids open, meeting Damian's hot, sleep-laden gaze.

Some part of me recalled his promise to give me a chance to turn him down when I was uncertain about letting him wake me up like this.

That part of me was a fucking moron.

I grabbed his hair and pulled him back down between my thighs, earning a low chuckle before he licked me again.

My hips arched and rocked as I panted and cursed. He lifted

me long enough to roll onto his back and pull me onto his face, like he'd mentioned so many times.

I lost control on his tongue twice—and then he finally gave me his cock.

Instead of taking me hard and fast, he drove into me slowly.

Deeply.

Intimately.

It was so, insanely intense.

And when we came together, I couldn't help but realize that we hadn't just screwed.

We'd made love.

And that was enough to make me want Damian even more.

Then again...

Had I ever not wanted him?

My lips curved upward.

Even when he'd pissed me off, I was still attracted to him.

We were made for each other—it was as simple and complicated as that.

epilogue

DAMIAN—A FEW MONTHS LATER

BLAIR WAS SITTING at her desk in our office, typing out an answer to an email, when I strode into the room.

She smiled as she turned to greet me—but her eyebrows lifted when she saw the gift bag in my hand.

"Who's that for?"

I set it on her lap. "Who do you think?"

"My birthday isn't for another two months," she protested. "And Christmas is still a few days away."

The tree in the corner of our office attested to that. Blair made sure we had all of Vamp Manor coated in Christmas décor since the day after Halloween, much to some people's horror and others' thrill.

It made her so happy that I took her side, every time.

If she wanted a few hundred—or thousand—trees, I'd buy the trees. And decorate them myself, if I had to.

Thankfully, I didn't have to.

And we had so many trees in our storage that we didn't have to buy any, so all I had to do was threaten a few Grinchy bastards to keep the complaints at a minimum.

"I'm tired of waiting. Open it," I said.

Her smile returned, and she pulled out the paper and peered into the bag.

Her forehead creased, and I bit back a grin as she pulled out the shiny black material. Her eyes narrowed when she realized what it was, and then met mine.

"A wetsuit, Damian? I told you, I'm not wearing a damn wetsuit."

"Take out everything else."

Her annoyance vanished as she pulled out two printed plane tickets—I'd had to create a fake version of them online, because the tickets were digital—and a far skimpier bikini than any of the ones she owned.

She scanned the tickets, and her eyes widened before they met mine once again. "You're taking me on vacation?"

"To the ocean," I agreed. "I rented a beach house tucked away in a cove with its own beach, so we can swim and walk around naked to your heart's content. The water's cold this time of year, though, if you have the misfortune of being a vampire."

She dropped the gift bag on the desk and threw her arms around me. When I lifted her off her feet, her legs wrapped around my waist too as she hugged me tightly. "The wetsuit is for *you?*"

"Mmhm. I promised to give you a wetsuit, but I didn't specify who would wear it."

She laughed against my skin. "I love you, Damian."

"I love you too, little siren." I kissed her forehead, but she pulled my face down to hers and captured my mouth.

I was so fucking glad that she was mine.

THE END

READ IZZY & PORTER'S STORY HERE

afterthoughts

Weird books are just so much fun.
I liked the idea of this book when I was planning on making
Blair human... but there was no passion. As soon as I
realized I wanted to make her a siren, with a side of
mermaid and a dash of vampirism.
Then, we were golden.
I legitimately wrote half of this book in two days. Two.
Days. The rest of it took longer—but the passion was still
there.
So, I guess I've learned my lesson.
Weird books are my thing.
Anyway, I am absolutely obsessed with Blair and Damian.
Obsessed. And I can't wait to see what happens with Izzy
and Porter, and the rest of the sirens too! Are we going to
have more ridiculously impossible pools? And more
chlorine?
Only time will tell ;)

Did I mention that the titles of the books in this series make me laugh every time? It's ridiculous.

I'm ridiculous.

But it's a heck of a lot of fun!

Anyway, thank you so much for reading! I hope you enjoyed this story as much as I do, and I hope you check out Izzy's book too.

Until next time!

All the love,

Lola Glass <3

stay in touch

If you want to receive Lola's newsletter for new releases (no spam!) use this link:

LINK

Or find her on:
FACEBOOK
TIKTOK
INSTAGRAM
PINTEREST
GOODREADS

all series by lola glass

Connected Standalones:

Mated to the King

Cub Lake Novellas

Survival of the Mated

Mate Mountain

Wildwood

Deceit & Devotion

Claimed by the Wolf

Forbidden Mates

Wild Hunt

Kings of Disaster

Night's Curse

Outcast Pack

Feral Pack

Mate Hunt

Series:

Burning Kingdom

Sacrificed to the Fae King

Shifter Queen

Wolfsbane

Shifter City

Supernatural Underworld

Moon of the Monsters

Rejected Mate Refuge

about the author

Lola is a book-lover with a *slight* romance obsession and a passion for love—real love. Not the flowers-and-chocolates kind of love, but the kind where two people build a relationship strong enough to last. That's the kind of relationship she loves to read about, and the kind she tries to portray in her books.

Even though they're fun stories about sassy women and huge, growly magical men ;)

www.ingramcontent.com/pod-product-compliance
Ingram Content Group UK Ltd.
Pitfield, Milton Keynes, MK11 3LW, UK
UKHW022311050225
454712UK00008B/26